Welcome to the Secret World of Alex Mack!

You should see the new Magic Emporium! It's incredible! It's got all kinds of magic tricks, and the salespeople are fantastic magicians. I didn't know anyone who liked it as much as my friend Ray, though. He was the one who learned—the hard way—that they were ripping off kids. When I found out about it, I decided it was time to turn the tables on those crooks with some tricks of our own. Let me explain. . . .

I'm Alex Mack. I was just another average kid until my first day of junior high.

One minute I'm walking home from school—the next there's a *crash!* A truck from the Paradise Valley Chemical plant overturns in front of me, and I'm drenched in some weird chemical.

And since then—well, nothing's been the same. I can move objects with my mind, shoot electrical charges through my fingertips, and morph into a liquid shape . . . which is handy when I get in a tight spot!

My best friend, Ray, thinks it's cool—and my sister, Annie, thinks I'm a science project.

They're the only two people who know about my new powers. I can't let anyone else find out—not even my parents—because I know the chemical plant wants to find me and turn me into some experiment.

But you know something? I guess I'm not so average anymore!

The Secret World of Alex Mack™

Available from MINSTREL Books

NICKELODEON®

the secret world of

ALEX MACK™

Hocus Pocus!

Joseph Locke

A MINSTREL® BOOK

Published by POCKET BOOKS
New York   London   Toronto   Sydney   Tokyo   Singapore

This book is a work of fiction. Names, characters, places and incidents are products of the author's imagination or are used fictitiously. Any resemblance to actual events or locales or persons, living or dead, is entirely coincidental.

A MINSTREL PAPERBACK *Original*

A Minstrel Book published by
POCKET BOOKS, a division of Simon & Schuster Inc.
1230 Avenue of the Americas, New York, NY 10020

ISBN: 0-671-00707-6

First Minstrel Books printing September 1997

10 9 8 7 6 5 4 3 2 1

Cover art by Thomas Queally and Pat Hill Studios

Printed in the U.S.A.

This book is for
Meredith Kanago

Hocus Pocus!

CHAPTER 1

"I don't know *why* my sister thinks I stole her favorite sweater," Alex Mack said as she walked with her best friend, Ray Alvarado, and Louis Driscoll. Louis lagged a pace or two behind, paying no attention to their conversation. He was too busy playing a hand-held video game.

It was a crisp fall Sunday, and they were on their way to the grand opening of the newest store in Paradise Valley: the St. Smythe Magic Emporium.

"Gee, Alex," Ray said, looking at her sideways, "I can't imagine why Annie'd think a thing like that. I've never known you to borrow your big sister's clothes," he finished sarcastically.

"Well, okay, maybe I have—once or twice," Alex

admitted. "But she's not talking to me now. I have to say, though, it was a great sweater, and it looked perfect on her. A beautiful peacock-blue cashmere-wool blend, soft as rose petals. It looked incredible on her, like it was made for her. Well, actually, it was made for her. It was a birthday gift our grandmother knitted, and it was Annie's absolute favorite piece of clothing."

"But was it *that* great?" Ray asked. "I mean, great enough to stop talking to you? After all, it's only a sweater."

"Well, it wasn't just any sweater, and umm, I borrowed it a lot, see. And I had it last." Alex tried to swallow the last few words so Ray wouldn't hear her confession, but he didn't miss a thing.

"Did you give it back?" Ray asked.

"Of course I did!" Alex replied emphatically. "She had a bunch of clothes folded and stacked on her bed. I figured it was a pile of fresh laundry, so I tossed the sweater on top of it. I don't know how she could have missed it."

"Don't worry," Ray said. "It'll turn up sooner or later. She'll realize her mistake, and the two of you will make up."

"I sure hope so."

They rounded the corner of the block and stopped to stare at the spectacle before them. Still immersed in his video game, Louis walked right into Ray, jabbing the hand-held game into the small of Ray's back and making him shout out and jump.

"This is some grand opening," Alex said.

Ray nodded and replied, "Yeah. I had no idea it would be *this* grand!"

In front of the St. Smythe Magic Emporium, a clown performed magic tricks for a group of youngsters and their parents. A nearby vendor was giving away hot dogs and soft drinks from a brightly colored cart.

"Why don't we wait a few days and come back after the crowd has thinned out?" Alex suggested.

Louis stuffed his video game into his back pocket, suddenly paying attention. "Aw, c'mon," he said. "Let's lose the clown and the kiddies and see what they've got in the store, huh?"

"Yeah, let's do that!" Ray said with a grin.

"Okay, okay," Alex agreed. "But remember, I can't stay long. I'm supposed to meet Nicole and Robyn."

"No problem," Ray said, pulling on her sleeve. "This won't take long." He led her into the store, with Louis following closely behind.

Before it was a magic store, the building had been a furniture showroom. Although the business had changed, the building was still cavernous inside. Instead of furniture, the store was filled with endless shelves and display cases of magic paraphernalia, novelties, and gag gifts.

The store was crowded with people of all ages. Behind the counters, employees demonstrated the merchandise by performing magic tricks for the amazed customers.

"Wow," Ray and Louis said simultaneously.

Alex gave them a sidelong glance, then shook her head. She didn't understand the attraction. "What's the big deal, Ray?" she asked. "You've never been into magic before."

Ray shrugged. "And I'm not now. I just thought it would be a cool place. And it is!"

"I'm not into magic, either," Louis said. "But I really want to get one of those rubber puddles of vomit. I'll catch up with you guys later." He hurried off toward a section of shelves beneath a large sign that read Practical Jokes and Novelties.

"I suppose you want to look around?" Alex asked Ray.

He grinned as he took her elbow in hand. "Yes, of course! Come on!" He led her into the store and they began to browse the merchandise on the shelves.

The St. Smythe Magic Emporium offered every

single magic trick Alex and Ray had ever seen performed by magicians on stage or on television, plus some tricks they'd never imagined. Even Alex grinned as they looked over the merchandise.

She stopped to inspect a "disappearing" bird-cage and checked the price tag. The price made her flinch. "Hey, Ray," she said. "If you're thinking of taking up magic as a hobby, I've got two words for you: very expensive!"

"Oh, no," Ray replied. "Not me. I'm saving up my money for a new bike for my paper route, remember? I'm not gonna be buying this stuff. I just thought this would be a fun store to browse through, that's all."

Alex laughed. "That's good to know," she said.

"Hey, look what I found!" Louis said suddenly.

Alex turned around and let out a yelp of fright. Just inches from her face, Louis held a squashed rat made of rubber. But at first glance, it had certainly looked real!

"Roadkill!" Louis said, bursting into delighted laughter.

Alex frowned. "Do that again, Louis, and you're gonna *be* roadkill!"

Still laughing, Louis turned and walked away.

With a sigh, Alex said to Ray, "As long as Louis

Driscoll has access to this store, Paradise Valley will not be a safe place to live."

Ray picked up a shiny black stick from one of the shelves. It was about eighteen inches long, with white tips. Smiling, he waved the wand over Alex's head and said, "Abracadabra! Hocus pocus!"

"A magic wand, huh?"

"Yeah!"

"What does it do?" Alex asked.

Ray inspected the wand carefully. "Well, nothing, I guess. It's just a prop."

"Then it's not much of a magic wand," Alex said, unimpressed.

As he held the wand, an idea began to form in Ray's head, and his dark eyes sparkled. He lowered his voice and whispered, "Hey, Alex, *you* could make this wand do something."

"Huh? What do you mean?"

"Just think about this a second. I could put on a magic show and charge admission, see. And all I'd really need would be this wand. Because you'd be there, behind the scenes, doing the *real* magic. You know, you could make things float, and—"

"Oh, no, Ray. Unh-unh." Alex folded her arms in front of her and stared at Ray levelly.

"C'mon, Alex, no one would ever know. You could hide in a—"

"No way. Forget it."

Ray sighed with disappointment.

"Think about what you're saying, Ray," Alex whispered. "My powers have been enough trouble as it is. Flaunting them like that would just be too risky."

"Yeah, you're right," Ray agreed with a nod. "Sorry. I'd never ask you to do anything like that. It was a stupid idea."

Alex smiled. "Not stupid, Ray. Just not all that . . . smart."

Ray turned to put the wand back on the shelf, but he stopped when a deep voice with a British accent spoke directly behind him. "A young magician's first magic wand is a very important decision," the man said.

Alex and Ray spun around to see a white-haired man with a goatee smiling down at them. His blue-gray eyes twinkled behind small, round eyeglasses. Beside him stood another man, husky and tall. His shoulders were broad and his chest deep. His dark hair was worn in a crewcut, and his face was expressionless. He wore a tight black turtleneck that displayed his bulging muscles.

Bowing ever so slightly at the waist, the white-haired man smoothly introduced himself: "Ethan St. Smythe, master of the magic arts and proprietor of this establishment. And this is my assistant, Mr. Burke."

Alex and Ray introduced themselves. Ray had forgotten that he still held the wand in his hand.

Mr. St. Smythe took the wand from Ray and held it between both hands. "This is an adequate model," he said, "if one is planning to take up magic merely as a hobby. But for the professional magician, it simply won't do." He clapped his hands together suddenly, and the wand disappeared!

Alex and Ray stared with wide eyes at the space where the wand had been just a second before.

"Now," Mr. St. Smythe continued, "if you're *serious* about magic—" He snapped the fingers of his left hand and, in the blink of an eye, another wand appeared in his right! "—*this* is the wand for you!" It was black, with silver tips, and had a glittery sheen to it. It was about six inches longer than the first wand.

"*Wow!*" Ray gasped. "How did you—"

Mr. St. Smythe silenced him by holding up a finger. "The first rule of magic, my boy: *never* reveal your secrets to anyone but another professional magician." He turned to Alex. "So, are you his assistant?"

"Oh, no," Alex said. "I'm just his friend. And, um . . ." She glanced at her watch. "If I don't take off now, I'm also going to be late. I'll see you later, okay, Ray?"

"Yeah, sure, Alex."

Mr. St. Smythe snapped his right wrist once. Out of nowhere, a colorful bouquet of silk flowers appeared in his hand. "For you, my dear. Please come again."

Alex felt herself blushing as she took the flowers. "Thank you, Mr. St. Smythe," she said with a grin. "I will come again!"

When Alex was gone, Mr. St. Smythe leaned toward Ray and murmured, "I couldn't help noticing you seemed rather embarrassed to discuss your interest in the magic arts in the presence of your friend."

"Oh, well, I wasn't really that interested in magic," Ray said, shrugging. "At least, I wasn't before I came in here."

"Ah. Then perhaps you're not yet ready for this particular model." Mr. St. Smythe held the glittering wand before him, blew on it once . . . and it disappeared into thin air, leaving behind only a few wisps of smoke.

Ray grinned and shook his head, amazed. He knew there was a trick to it, a secret, but on the surface, it was almost as if Mr. St. Smythe had extraordinary powers, just like Alex.

"But you are a little interested in the magic arts, I presume."

"Well, yes, now I am," Ray said.

"Good. That's all it takes, my boy. A little interest in the magic arts is more valuable than all the college degrees in the world! Isn't that right, Mr. Burke?"

The enormous man nodded silently.

"Why is that, Mr. St. Smythe?" Ray asked.

"My boy, have you any idea what a career in the magic arts can get you?"

Ray shook his head. Mr. St. Smythe reached down and touched Ray's ear. Ray heard something rustle softly. When he pulled his hand back, Mr. St. Smythe held a dollar bill in it. "It can get you a lot of these, Ray, my boy." He stuffed the dollar into Ray's shirt pocket. "Keep that. After all, it came out of your ear."

"But before you can make any money at it, doesn't it take years and years of practice?" Ray asked.

"Magic? Not if you have a good teacher. That's why I set up the Young Magicians' Society. To give eager young magicians like yourself a good solid start."

"The Young Magicians' Society?" Ray asked thoughtfully. "Can anyone join? I mean, how can I join?"

"With a simple entry fee of seventy-nine dollars and ninety-five cents, you may begin your lessons."

Ray thought it over. He'd saved up forty dollars for his bike. . . .

Before either of them could continue, Louis approached Ray, carrying a bag of purchases. "I'm ready to go whenever you are, Ray," he said.

"I'll be with you in a minute, Louis," Ray said. "Go look around some more."

Louis walked away with an agreeable shrug.

"Once you begin to learn the secrets of the magic arts, Ray, my boy," Mr. St. Smythe went on in a low, conspiratorial tone, "you can perform for friends. When word of your talent gets around, you'll be in demand at parties and banquets. Then, perhaps a local theater or two. Before you know it, Ray, you're performing at Carnegie Hall to riotous applause . . . and the money is rolling in!"

Ray chewed on his lip, imagining himself performing before a cheering, clapping audience. All the kids in school were there, even some of the girls who were older, and they were completely amazed. After a moment, he said, "No offense, Mr. St. Smythe, but why should I believe you? I mean, you can obviously do some pretty neat tricks, but what qualifies you to teach me all about the magic arts?"

Mr. St. Smythe's eyebrows rose and his mouth curled in a half smile. "I like caution, Ray. It shows common sense, and that's good. Come with me, and I will answer your question."

Ray went with Mr. St. Smythe and Mr. Burke to the back of the store and down a dimly lit corridor. They entered a spacious room where large cardboard boxes were stacked against the walls. The room had a gritty, dirty concrete floor that was littered with gum wrappers and smashed cigarette and cigar butts. In the middle of the room was a round table with four chairs positioned around it. There was a deck of cards on the tabletop.

The silent Mr. Burke went to the table and took a seat. He produced a cigar as if from thin air and lit it. A cloud of bluish smoke formed around his head as he clenched the cigar between his teeth. Mr. Burke picked up the cards and began manipulating them with surprising grace and agility. They flew back and forth between his big hands, fanned out, folded up, and danced over his knuckles, all with little apparent effort from the huge man.

Putting a hand on Ray's shoulder, Mr. St. Smythe led him to a poster on the wall. It featured a black-and-white photograph of a man in a black suit, black cape, and top hat, holding a long black-and-white magic wand. At the top of the poster, bold letters spelled out The Magnificent St. Smythe!

"Is that you?" Ray asked.

"That's correct, young man. I performed twice for the Royal Family. I was, for a time, considered the greatest magician in all of Europe. But that was when I wore a younger man's clothes, Ray. Today I am content to pass my knowledge on to young people such as yourself, to keep alive the secrets of the magic arts."

Ray stared at the poster and imagined himself wearing such a suit and cape, standing on a stage and performing magic.

"So, Ray, my boy, are you interested in joining the Young Magicians' Society?"

Ray was about to agree wholeheartedly, but then he remembered the entry fee. Ray's heart sank. He wondered how long it would take him to make up the difference. If he worked hard at odd jobs all over town, sold some of his comic books and collectible cards . . . Actually, it might not take very long at all! "I want to join, Mr. St. Smythe," he said. "But I don't have the money right now."

"Oh, do not misunderstand me, Ray. I am not pressuring you, not at all. If you have the money, fine. If not, that's fine, too. Perhaps later, when you can afford it, you can join—if there are any openings left."

"Any openings left?" Ray asked, feeling a tinge of panic in his chest.

"You see, I can only take on a limited number of students at a time," Mr. St. Smythe said. "As you know, we're new here in Paradise Valley, but the Young Magicians' Society tends to fill up rather quickly."

"Oh, I see," Ray said, frowning. He wondered how he could make enough money to join the society before it filled up and decided that somehow he would. "I'm going to work hard to make the money I need to join, Mr. St. Smythe. And as soon as I have it, I'll come pay the entry fee."

"Fine, that's fine, Ray," Mr. St. Smythe said with a smile. "But don't wait till you have the money to come back. You're welcome here anytime at all. Feel free to drop in for a visit. The door is always open."

On the way out of the store, Louis got a hot dog. As he and Louis walked, Louis ate and chattered on and on about the wonderful stuff he'd seen in the store. Ray barely heard his friend. He was too preoccupied with the Young Magicians' Society.

With nearly forty dollars left to make, he would have to work hard before he could afford to join. But he continued to imagine himself performing for a large applauding audience . . . and something else, something even more appealing.

Ray's best friend in the world, Alex, was imbued with powers that had come to her purely by accident. They were great powers, superhuman powers, but she'd gotten them by chance when a truck had spilled a bizarre and illegal chemical on her, GC-161. Secretly Ray had always envied those wonderful powers. Alex had to keep her abilities a secret, of course, because the people at the Paradise Valley Chemical plant would snatch her up the moment she was discovered as the kid who'd been doused with the GC-161. But to have such powers, to be able to do things no other person on earth could possibly do, and do them publicly, anytime at all . . .

If Ray became a member of the Young Magicians' Society, he would learn things that would allow him to at least appear as if he had such powers. He could appear to do many of the same things Alex could do and he wouldn't have to keep it a secret. After all, what good was keeping your magical powers secret? That ruined half the fun!

He could show off to all the kids at school. Impress his father with how hard he'd studied to learn the magical skills. Maybe even enter and win a competition!

For that, Ray thought it would be worth whatever it took to raise the money needed.

CHAPTER 2

Three days after the grand opening of St. Smythe's Magic Emporium, Alex caught up with Ray in front of the school building after her last class.

"Hey, Ray," she said. "I have to go to the library and check out a couple of books for a research paper I'm writing. Why don't you come along with me and we can go get a milk shake after, or something?"

Ray gave her a halfhearted smile. "I'd like to, Alex, but I can't. I've got some, uh, just some stuff to do."

"Okay." They walked along silently for a few moments before Alex asked, "Hey, Ray, is everything all right?"

"Sure, Alex, everything's fine. Why?"

"Well, I haven't seen much of you the last few days. As soon as school's out, you disappear. So I started wondering if something was wrong."

"No, nothing's wrong, Alex. I'm just busy, that's all. In fact, I've gotta be someplace in a few minutes. Maybe we can get together this weekend, okay?"

"Yeah, sure, Ray," Alex said. She waved as he hurried across the street and disappeared around a corner.

Walking on by herself, Alex couldn't help wondering what was up with her friend.

What was up with Ray was work.

After leaving St. Smythe's Magic Emporium on Sunday afternoon, Ray had made up his mind to earn the thirty-nine dollars and change he needed to join the Young Magicians' Society, no matter how hard he had to work. That day, he'd gone from neighborhood to neighborhood, from door to door, asking people if there was any work he could do for them.

Ray had found odd jobs all over town. For the last three days, he'd gone straight from his paper route, to school, to a job, and from that job to yet another. He'd mowed Mr. and Mrs. Ackerman's front lawn on Monday. After that, he'd put on some old clothes and painted the picket fence that surrounded Mr. Hathaway's small front yard. When he was finished painting, he went over to Mrs. Mesner's house to clean out her garage. Mrs. Mesner was a widow with three children, and she had a very messy garage. It was a big job, and he'd had to go back on Tuesday to finish up. But she'd given him five dollars and made a batch of delicious brownies!

On Tuesday, after finishing up at Mrs. Mesner's, he'd gone to Mr. Ratchett's house. Mr. Ratchett was a frail old man confined to a wheelchair. His daughter, who usually did his grocery shopping twice a week, had gone out of town. So after school, Ray had gotten the list from Mr. Ratchett and gone to the grocery store a few blocks away to do his shopping. Then he'd gone to Mr. Grimhoff's candy store and newsstand and washed the store's windows. The young man who usually washed Mr. Grimhoff's windows had gone into the hospital to have his appendix removed, so Ray had gotten the job.

Ray never knew how much he was going to be paid for his work. Some people paid more than others, but Ray didn't mind. Whether it was a little or a lot, it meant he was closer to his goal.

He'd told none of his friends about what he was doing, and he felt guilty for keeping it from them, especially after seeing the concern in Alex's eyes. But he knew if he told them he was trying to raise money to join the Young Magicians' Society, they would laugh—Alex, Louis, Nicole, Robyn, all of them. They wouldn't do it to be cruel, of course, but they would, no doubt, think he was making a big mistake. They would see it as just another one of his moneymaking schemes and would try to talk him out of it.

So Ray had decided to keep it to himself. He didn't want to tell them until he was able to pay the entry fee and had gotten a few lessons from Mr. St. Smythe. Then he wouldn't have to *tell* his friends, he could *show* them. That way, they wouldn't be able to laugh, and they'd be so impressed, they wouldn't think of discouraging him!

Working so many jobs was taking a toll, even after only a few days. Ray got home late each night, and after eating a warmed-up dinner, he had homework to do. As a result, he'd been getting to bed later than usual, which was making him tired.

After leaving Alex on Wednesday, he headed to the house of an elderly woman named Mrs. Draper to trim her hedges and pull the weeds that had grown up around them. But after that, he had no new jobs lined up.

That was beginning to worry him. When he was done at Mrs. Draper's house, Ray planned to look around for more work. But Paradise Valley wasn't a very big town, and he'd covered nearly every neighborhood. It wouldn't be so bad if he could take his time to make the money, but he was afraid the Young Magicians' Society would fill up before he was able to pay his entry fee!

Each afternoon, between jobs, Ray dropped by the St. Smythe Magic Emporium and spent a few minutes visiting with Mr. St. Smythe. Mostly, he wanted to find out if the society had filled up yet. But he also enjoyed watching Mr. St. Smythe perform his magic tricks.

On Monday, Mr. St. Smythe had put a colorful box on Mr. Burke's head. It locked in the front and completely covered Mr. Burke's head and neck. Then, Mr. St. Smythe inserted a long, sinister-looking knife into each of the box's four sides. The blades went all the way through, until the tips showed on the opposite sides. A moment later, Mr. St. Smythe removed the knives and opened the box to reveal Mr. Burke's head . . . untouched and unharmed.

On Tuesday, Mr. St. Smythe had plucked a shiny

red ball from out of the air. Next he'd turned it into two balls, then three, then four. He made the balls dance over his knuckles for a few moments, then made them disappear one at a time, until there were none left.

After each trick, Mr. St. Smythe said to Ray, "Once you become a member of the Young Magicians' Society, you'll be performing illusions like these in no time at all. After a while, they'll become second nature to you. And before you know it, you'll be a master of the magic arts!"

With each of Mr. St. Smythe's reminders, Ray could almost hear the sound of applause from an enthusiastic audience. He could almost feel what it might be like to have the kind of supernatural powers that Alex possessed. . . .

Almost.

From Mrs. Draper's house, Ray went door-to-door again, inquiring about work. After ninety minutes, he hadn't found a single job. Feeling disappointed and tired, Ray went to the St. Smythe Magic Emporium. Although it wasn't as busy as it had been on the day of the grand opening, there were always plenty of customers in the store, browsing the shelves and watching the employees perform.

"Ray, my boy!" Mr. St. Smythe called from behind the front counter as Ray opened the shop's door. "You're just in time for a piece of candy!"

When Ray walked over to him, Mr. St. Smythe gestured toward an ornately carved and colorfully painted box on the countertop.

"Chocolate doves," Mr. St. Smythe said. "Help yourself."

Ray opened the hinged lid of the box. Inside were rows of delicate-looking chocolate doves with their wings spread. He removed one, then closed the lid.

Mr. St. Smythe passed his hand over the box with a flourish and said, "Or perhaps you would prefer *white* chocolate doves!" He nodded for Ray to open the box again.

All of the chocolate doves inside had turned a creamy white.

"That's amazing!" Ray said, closing the lid again.

"Better yet," Mr. St. Smythe said, passing both hands over the box this time. "The real thing!"

When Ray opened the box a third time, four live white doves flew out, their wings nearly coming close enough to brush his face. Ray laughed as he watched them fly to the highest shelf in the store and settle there, cooing softly. "Incredible!" he exclaimed.

Mr. St. Smythe chuckled with satisfaction. "Just another of the illusions you'll be performing someday soon, Ray, my boy. At least, I *hope* it's soon. The Young Magicians' Society is filling up awfully fast."

Ray's smile melted away. "Really? There are openings left, though, aren't there?"

"For now. But they will be snatched up very soon, I have no doubt. It's not my policy to reserve positions in the society, I'm afraid. It's first pay, first serve. So, have you managed to obtain any money, Ray?"

"Well, yes, I—I've been working hard all week. But I still don't have enough."

Mr. St. Smythe clicked his tongue and shook his head. "That's too bad. Ah, well, you can only do your best. Keep trying, Ray. Who knows? You might raise the money in time."

Ray left the store feeling heavy with disappointment. He'd hoped he wouldn't have to do it, but Ray feared he was going to have to go to his father for help. Maybe Dad would have some work Ray could do around the house for a few extra bucks. If he wasn't able to find some more jobs the next day, Ray decided he would have no choice but to approach his dad.

He wanted so much to be a member of the Young Magicians' Society. He knew he could become an accomplished, successful magician with Mr. St. Smythe's help. But he was running out of jobs . . . and he was running out of time!

CHAPTER 3

After school on Thursday, Ray picked up Mr. Ratchett's grocery shopping list, then went to the store. He wanted to get the shopping out of the way so he could start looking for more work right away. In the store, Ray carried a red plastic grocery basket in his right hand and Mr. Ratchett's list in his left as he went up and down the aisles, filling the basket.

"Ray!"

Startled, Ray spun around to see Louis rushing toward him with his hand held out to shake. Although he thought it was kind of dorky, Ray shook Louis's hand . . . and felt a jittering vibration against his palm! The buzzing sensation was so surprising, Ray stumbled backward, tripped over his own feet, and fell to the floor. The contents of the basket scattered around him. Oranges and canned goods went rolling, and Ray felt a squashed box of doughnuts under his elbow.

Holding up his right hand, Louis doubled over with laughter. There was a round metal device attached to his middle finger. "I couldn't resist!" Louis said, gasping for air. "Hey, you know what? That new magic store is *great!*" Still laughing, Louis gathered up the spilled groceries, put them in the basket, and helped Ray to his feet.

"It's a good thing there was nothing breakable in there, you bozo!" Ray said, brushing himself off.

"What're you doing here, anyway?" Louis asked. "You've got a grocery store just a block from your house."

"Oh, umm, I'm just getting some groceries for someone. It's a job, that's all."

"A job, huh? Still trying to make enough money to buy a new bike?"

Ray nodded, trying not to wince at the small lie. "Yeah, that's it. It's, uh, for the bike."

"Is that what you've been up to all week?" Louis asked. "Because we've been wondering about you."

"We? We *who?*"

"Well, me, Alex, Nicole, Robyn—you remember us, don't you? Your *friends?*"

"I'm sorry. I've just been really busy, I swear. Maybe I'll see you guys this weekend."

"Sure, that'd be great. As long as you're just working and . . . well, nothing's wrong, or anything. We've been kind of worried about you."

"Don't worry," Ray said with a smile. "I'm fine."

Louis gave Ray's shoulder a genial punch and said, "Well, I guess I'll see you later, huh?"

"Yeah, later," Ray said as his friend hurried away. Once Louis was out of sight, Ray released a long, heavy sigh, then continued shopping for Mr. Ratchett's groceries. He finally knew how Alex felt, having to lie to her friends all the time about her powers. He'd just lied right to Louis's face about why he was working all the time. And it wasn't a good feeling.

By the end of the day, Ray had found no new jobs, although he'd spent nearly three hours hunting. He decided not to pay a visit to Mr. St. Smythe; it was just too embarrassing to show up when he still didn't have enough money to join the Young Magicians' Society. Instead, Ray went straight home. He arrived early enough to have dinner with his dad for the first time all week.

Ray and Mr. Alvarado exchanged small talk over

dinner, but in his head, Ray was rehearsing his question over and over, until he finally found the right moment to bring it up.

"Hey, Dad," he said, "you wouldn't happen to have any work I could do around the house, would you? I mean, things you haven't had time to do yourself?"

Mr. Alvarado smiled. "So, *that's* where you've been every night this week, huh? Out working to raise money for your bike?"

Ray didn't want to lie to his dad, so he just smiled and mumbled, "Well, yeah, I've been trying to come up with some extra money, Dad."

"I'm glad to see you working hard to earn your own money, Ray," Mr. Alvarado said. "It shows maturity and responsibility. And you know I'd help you out if I could. But I'm afraid I can't this time. The car's transmission is about to give out on me. It'll have to be replaced. That's going to be expensive, and it'll take a chunk out of our budget."

Ray was disappointed, though he knew his father would help him out if he could.

"But don't worry, Ray," Mr. Alvarado said. "Remember, your birthday is just around the corner. Maybe something will turn up." He gave Ray a cheerful wink.

That night, after finishing his homework, Ray lay

awake in bed later than usual. He couldn't stop wondering if perhaps more openings in the Young Magicians' Society had been filled since he'd spoken with Mr. St. Smythe the day before . . . if there were still any openings left.

When he finally slept, Ray dreamed of being onstage and performing elaborate illusions that Alex could never, ever perform in public . . . and doing it all for an audience that showed its delight and approval with wild applause.

After school on Friday, Ray had no job to go to. He had gone to nearly every house in Paradise Valley looking for work, only to find none. But he wasn't going to let that get him down; things could change tomorrow. In the meantime, he walked home with Alex. She talked about school and complained about Annie's persistent silence. But Ray heard only part of it. His mind was elsewhere, wondering if there was any room left for him in the Young Magicians' Society.

"Okay, Ray," Alex said suddenly, firmly. *"Something* is wrong, and I want you to tell me what it is. I've been worried about you all week. Louis said you've been doing odd jobs to make money for your bike, but there must be something else! You seem so bummed!"

Ray sighed heavily. He was reluctant to tell her the truth because he was afraid she'd laugh and say the whole thing was a horrible idea. He certainly wasn't going to tell her that part of his motivation for joining the Young Magicians' Society was so he could have "powers" of his own, just like her. That sounded so . . . silly . . . even though it was true.

But Ray wanted to tell somebody, and who better than his best friend? So he told her all about the Young Magicians' Society and how much he could learn from Mr. St. Smythe if he could just pay the initial fee.

Alex cocked her head and frowned slightly. "But I thought you were saving up for a new bike for your paper route," she said.

"Well, I was. But think about it, Alex. Once I learn all this stuff, I can start earning money by doing magic shows, and then I can afford to buy a better bike than I ever could with the money I was saving."

"Well, if you think it's a good idea, Ray . . ." She sounded cautious.

"You think it's a bad idea," Ray said, his shoulders sagging.

"No, no, I didn't say that. I just think that when

it comes to that much money, you should be careful."

"So . . . you think it's a bad idea?"

She smiled. "I didn't say that. If it's what you want to do, Ray, I think it's great. Really. Hey, maybe if you get good enough, we'll both be able to make things levitate," she added with a laugh.

"You know, that crossed my mind," Ray said with a sheepish chuckle.

"Really?"

"Well, yeah, I thought it'd be kinda neat if . . . you know, if I had some magical powers like you. Even though mine would be . . . well, you know . . . fake."

Alex laughed. "You're right! That *would* be kinda neat!"

Ray's smile disappeared. "The only problem is, I can't seem to find any more work. Looks like I've used up all the odd jobs in Paradise Valley."

"Well . . ." Alex thought a moment as they walked. "You know, Nicole and Robyn have been worried about you, too. Maybe we can all help you out. We're getting together tomorrow to help Nicole with her newest project. We're going to be folding and stapling flyers for the Humane Society."

"Flyers?"

"Yeah. They're to remind everyone to have their dogs and cats spayed and neutered. We're meeting at my place for lunch, around noon. Why don't you join us?"

Cheered by the prospect of a new job, Ray smiled. "Yeah, sure! I'd love to! Thanks! But, umm, could we keep this just between us? I mean about me joining the Magicians' Society."

"Sure."

"Thanks, Alex."

Alex returned his smile. "Don't worry, Ray. We'll conjure up something," she said as she stopped walking. After a quick glance around to make sure no one was watching, Alex waved her hand in the direction of a clump of weeds on the ground; the weeds had tiny mustard-yellow flowers on them. As if pulled out of the ground by an invisible hand, the weeds rose and floated over to Ray, who plucked them out of the air. In her best impression of Mr. St. Smythe's deep, accented voice, Alex said, "For you, my dear, a fragrant bouquet of freshly picked weeds!"

They laughed as they walked on. Ray moved with more of a spring in his step. Maybe Alex was right. Maybe they *would* conjure up something.

CHAPTER 4

First thing Saturday morning, Mr. Mack went to the plant to take care of some unfinished work left over from the week. Mrs. Mack left at the same time for the local library to help set up for a used book sale to raise money to buy new books.

So it was just Alex and Annie in the kitchen.

As Alex ate her breakfast—a bowl of hot oatmeal and a banana—Annie busied herself making a bowl of cold cereal, getting a glass of orange juice. And, of course, she never spoke to Alex. Not even when Alex said, "Good morning." Annie finished her breakfast first and silently went up to the bedroom she shared with Alex.

When she was finished eating, Alex washed her

breakfast dishes, then headed for the bedroom. The door was closed and she could hear music playing inside. She stood outside the bedroom a moment, wondering if she should confront Annie and try to put this ugly business behind them. Finally, she walked into the bedroom and stood at the foot of Annie's bed.

Annie was lying on her bed, propped up on one elbow. A binder and textbook were open before her, surrounded by a few loose pages. She glanced up when the door opened, but quickly returned her attention to her work.

Alex took a deep breath and said, "Annie, I think we should talk about this."

"About what?"

"About your sweater."

"Why? You'll give it back when your conscience bothers you long enough."

"Annie, I didn't take it. I *told* you, I put it on your bed. I would never steal anything of yours. I mean, sure, I liked to borrow it and wear it, but I wouldn't *steal* it. I just wouldn't *do* anything like that!"

Annie looked at her. "Okay, then where is it?"

"Well, it's gotta be around here someplace!"

"I've already searched everywhere." Annie looked down at her book again.

"But you can't just—"

Alex stopped talking when Annie reached over and turned up the stereo's volume so that the music drowned out her voice.

With a frustrated sigh, Alex folded her arms across her chest. She possessed the powers of a comic-book superhero, but she was powerless to make Annie believe that she hadn't stolen the sweater.

Moving with determination, Alex went to her closet. It was a mess, but it was her mess, so she understood it. She turned the closet upside down looking for Annie's sweater. When she didn't find it, she crossed the room to Annie's closet.

"Hey," Annie said, raising her voice to be heard above the music, "what're you doing?"

"I'm looking for your sweater."

"I've already looked there."

"Well, I'm looking again!"

But the sweater wasn't there.

Alex looked under both beds and in all the drawers. The sweater was not in the bedroom. She left the bedroom, went downstairs, and looked underneath every piece of furniture in the living room. From there, she went to the laundry room, where she went through the clothes in the hamper. The sweater was nowhere in the house.

That left her parents' bedroom, and they didn't strike her as sweater-stealing types.

Alex flopped into her dad's recliner with a groan. She knew she hadn't kept the sweater, and if Annie hadn't seen it, and it was nowhere in the house . . . then where had it gone?

Mrs. Mack returned an hour before Nicole, Robyn, and Ray arrived, and she prepared a lunch of grilled cheese sandwiches and tomato soup. The meal perfectly complemented the biting autumn chill outside. The three girls chattered over lunch, but Ray only nodded, smiled, and gave them an occasional brief response.

After finishing their lunch, they cleared the table. Alex brought a boom box into the dining room and turned on some music as Nicole spread out the pages of the flyers, along with two staplers. The four of them began to fold and staple the flyers methodically, industriously. And all the while, they talked and laughed.

"Hey, Ray," Nicole said, "where've you been lately, anyway? We haven't seen you all week. Is everything okay?"

"Sure," Ray said. "Everything's cool. I've just been busy doing odd jobs around town, trying to make some extra money."

Robyn leaned forward and whispered, "I hope you haven't gotten yourself involved in any criminal activity!"

"Of course he hasn't, Robyn!" Nicole replied.

"He's just been doing some jobs around town, that's all," Alex said.

"Jobs around town?" Robyn said. "That's exactly how it starts. This is classic gangster activity. We're talking organized crime, here!"

Nicole turned to Robyn and said, "You've been watching too many true-crime shows, girl!"

Ray laughed, and raised his hands as if he'd just been caught by the police. "I swear I'm not a criminal, officer," he said. "I've just been mowing lawns, trimming hedges, that sort of thing. But it's starting to look like I've managed to squeeze the last of the odd jobs out of Paradise Valley in only a week. All of a sudden, I can't find any work. That's why I'm glad you invited me to come help you with this. I need all the money I can get."

The three girls froze and stared at one another for a long moment. Then they burst into laughter.

Puzzled, Ray's eyes widened as he looked at his three friends. "What? What did I say? What's so funny?"

"This is volunteer work, Ray," Alex said.

He nodded once. "Yeah, so?"

"So," Nicole replied, "that means we're volunteering our time for *free*."

"We don't get paid for this, Ray," Alex added. "I thought you knew that."

Ray slumped in his chair. "Sorry, I guess I just . . . misunderstood you. My fault."

Alex placed a reassuring hand on Ray's arm. "Don't worry, you'll find some more work. Maybe we can help."

"Yeah," Nicole said, "there's got to be something else out there."

Robyn frowned thoughtfully for a moment, then said, "You know, Ray, I could use some help with my dog-walking business the next couple of days. It's not a lot of money, but it's something. I mean, if you don't mind walking dogs." She looked hopefully at him.

Ray brightened a little. "No, I don't mind at all! Thanks, Robyn. When will you need me?"

"This afternoon, soon as we're done here."

"No problem!" Ray said.

"Hey, my dad might be able to give you some work," Alex said.

"Really? What kind?" Ray chuckled. "Not that it matters. I'm just curious."

"Well, he's been tinkering with the lawn mower the last few weeks. He says he's 'improving it.'

You know Dad. Anyway, he's been too busy at work to try it out. He'd probably give you a few bucks to mow the front and back lawns."

"That would be great!" Ray said, brightening even more.

"I'll ask him this afternoon."

Nicole smiled across the table at Ray. "See? You should always come to your friends first. Four heads are better than one!"

Alex reached over and playfully poked Ray in the ribs, making him start and laugh. "Don't worry," she said. "You'll have money hanging out of your pockets in no time."

Ray smiled as he continued folding the flyers and passing them to Alex to be stapled. He couldn't wait to perform some dazzling illusions for Alex, Nicole, Robyn, and Louis. But first, he had to become a member of the Young Magicians' Society so he could begin to learn from Mr. St. Smythe. With his friends' help, that might happen sooner than he'd thought!

CHAPTER 5

Ray had been worried he wasn't going to find any more work, so he was happy to be busy again. And he was *very* busy for the rest of the weekend. When all the Humane Society flyers were folded, stapled, and boxed, Ray joined Robyn to walk some dogs.

"I walk a couple of Great Danes three times a week," Robyn explained as they started down the block. "Not only are they huge, but they're so playful that they're almost more than I can handle alone. On Saturdays, I also have to walk three poodles, a Shelty, and two boxers. I can walk the Shelty and the boxers at the same time, but then I have to walk the poodles, and then the Great

Danes. With you to help me, I can walk the poodles while you walk the Great Danes, then we can go back and get the Shelty and the boxers. That way, I can do it in two trips, instead of three."

"Sounds easy enough," Ray said. "Where do we take the dogs when we get them?"

"To the park," Robyn said, turning up a walkway that led to a brick house. "We'll walk them all the way around the park once, then take them back home."

They stopped to pick up the poodles first. The dogs' owner, a little old lady named Mrs. Benechek, waved good-bye as Robyn took the dogs away on their leashes. The three white poodles were identical, and to tell them apart, Mrs. Benechek had put ribbons on their ears. Dolly wore red ribbons, Daisy wore blue ribbons, and Dot wore green ones.

Robyn and Ray walked a few more blocks to get the Great Danes, Butch and Zeke. They were huge black and white dogs, and they loved Ray! The second they saw him, the two big, lumbering dogs bounded off the porch and jumped up on Ray, knocking him on his behind. The dogs frantically licked his face as he sputtered and coughed. Robyn tried not to laugh but couldn't help herself.

Once Ray was on his feet and had a firm hold

on the two leashes, he and Robyn headed for the park. On the way, the Great Danes kept trying to jump up on Ray and lick his face. When they weren't doing that, they tried to play with the three poodles, sending the little white dogs into fits of fearful whimpering.

To separate the poodles from the overly enthusiastic Great Danes, Robyn walked ahead of Ray rather than beside him. With the poodles out of reach, the Great Danes turned their attention to Ray again, trying to smother him with their playful affection.

When they reached the park, Ray and Robyn began to walk the five dogs around the park's perimeter. Robyn stayed several paces ahead of Ray to keep the Great Danes from terrorizing the timid poodles. The park's lush green grass was covered with brittle orange leaves, and the chilly autumn breeze made even more leaves flutter down from the trees. Behind Ray, a squirrel scurried down one of the tree trunks, then over the leaf-scattered grass . . . just a few feet from Butch and Zeke.

The two Great Danes erupted in a fit of barking as they bounded forward to chase the squirrel. Caught off guard, Ray found himself suddenly flat on the ground and being dragged over the grass by the huge dogs.

Ray shouted, "Butch! Zeke! Stop! Heel! Whoah!"

He finally bent a knee and was able to anchor himself enough to pull back on the two leashes. The Great Danes came to a halt but continued to bark as the squirrel made its getaway.

"Are you all right, Ray?" Robyn asked.

"I'm fine."

As Ray got to his feet and brushed himself off, Robyn noticed that the Great Danes were in reach of the poodles. Butch and Zeke noticed at the same time!

"Oh, no!" Robyn cried, trying to pull the poodles away. But she was too late.

The Great Danes dove forward and began to lick the poodles' faces with their big pink tongues and batted at the poodles playfully with their mittlike paws.

Ray shouted, "Heel, Butch! Zeke! Stop!" He pulled on the leashes until the Great Danes finally backed away from the trembling, but unhurt, poodles. "I'm sorry, Robyn!" he said.

But Robyn wasn't looking at him . . . she was staring down at the ground with wide eyes and an open mouth.

When Ray followed her gaze, he saw that all the poodles' identifying ribbons were scattered over the grass.

"Oh, no!" Ray cried. "Robyn, do you remember which poodle is which?"

She turned to him, her eyes still wide. "No . . . do *you*?"

Ray shook his head.

Robyn took a deep breath, then said, "Okay, okay. I'll do my best." She gathered up the ribbons, sat on the ground, and began tying them to the poodles' ears. When she was done, she stood, looked at Ray, and said, "I sure hope I'm right."

After walking around the park once, they took Butch and Zeke home first because they were so rambunctious. Ray was glad to be rid of them. "I think you deserve a raise for taking care of those big guys," he said to Robyn.

When they took the poodles home, Mrs. Benechek was waiting for them on the front porch. As Ray and Robyn left, they heard Mrs. Benechek talking to her dogs: "It's snacktime, babies! Here, Dolly, this is yours. . . . No, no, Daisy, that *Dolly's!* This one is for you, Daisy! No, not *you*, Dot, that's *Daisy's!*"

Ray and Robyn hurried down the sidewalk before Mrs. Benechek became suspicious.

On their way to pick up the Shelty and the boxers, Robyn said, "Tomorrow's my mom's birthday, and we're throwing a party for her. Would you mind walking some dogs for me, Ray?"

"No, not at all," Ray said, secretly hoping they weren't Great Danes.

"You can probably do it in one trip," she said. "It's two beagles and three chihuahuas."

Ray smiled and released a sigh of relief. "Oh, that sounds easy enough. Sure, I can do that."

"Good!" Robyn said. "I'll give you the address. You can pick the dogs up around ten tomorrow morning. I really appreciate it, Ray."

"Hey, it's no problem at all!" Ray said.

Robyn and Ray walked the Shelty and boxers around the park with no difficulty. After they took the dogs back home, Ray went back to Alex's house to see about mowing the lawn. The "improved" mower was waiting for him on the front lawn, and Alex met him at the front door.

"Dad said he'd love it if you mowed the lawn," Alex said. "He revved up the engine and lowered the blade a little, so it should work really well. He's working in his office right now, but he said to go ahead and start as soon as you got here."

"Great!" Ray said with a smile.

Alex sat on the front porch and watched as Ray pushed the mower to a front corner of the yard, then put a foot on the back wheel and pulled on the cord to start the motor. He had to pull it a few times, but it finally roared to life.

Ray got behind the mower and gripped the handle, ready to push it forward . . . when something strange began to happen.

At first, a spray of shredded grass shot from the mower's discharge, which was normal. But then, a chunk of brown dirt flew from the discharge, followed by another . . . and another, and another, and another!

The motor began to slow as great clots of earth—more and more of them—began to shoot from beneath the mower. As the motor slowed, black smoke began to rise from the mower.

"Oh, no!" Alex cried out.

"Oh, no!" Ray echoed. He reached down and hit the lever that turned off the mower. Once the motor had died, he got behind the machine, lifted a bit on the handle, and pushed it forward.

The mower had left behind a round hole in the lawn.

Ray turned to Alex and said, "I think your dad might have lowered the blade just a little too much."

Alex went inside and got Mr. Mack. After inspecting the hole in the ground, Mr. Mack said, "I think I might have lowered the blade just a little too much."

Mr. Mack told Ray to come back the next day, after he'd had a chance to fix the problem. After a day of Great Danes and poodles and a mower with a dirt-eating blade, Ray was more than happy to go home.

But he went back to Alex's house on Sunday. Once again, the mower was waiting for him on the front lawn.

"Dad raised the blade," Alex said, "so it shouldn't chew up the ground this time. In fact, with the revved-up motor, he said you shouldn't have to go over the same patch of lawn twice." She smiled and sat down on the porch to watch as Ray approached the mower.

The motor started with one swift pull of the cord. Ray stepped behind the mower and reached out to grip the handle, but . . . the mower rolled away from him on its own!

"Hey!" Ray shouted.

"Hey!" Alex shouted. She stood, pounded on the front door with her fist, and cried, "Dad! Dad, get out here!"

The mower jittered and rolled over the lawn and onto the sidewalk. It roared down the sidewalk, leaving a trail of gas fumes behind.

"C'mon, let's stop it!" Alex cried, breaking into a run.

Ray and Alex ran after the runaway mower together as it glided along the sidewalk rapidly, its chrome handle jiggling up and down.

Alex stopped suddenly and clenched her teeth as she concentrated hard, reaching out with her telekinetic powers. As the lawn mower jerked to a halt, its motor growled against the invisible force field that suddenly held it.

Ray hurried to the mower's side, reached down, and hit the lever, turning it off.

"Wow!" Alex said with a sigh as she approached Ray. "I hope Dad hasn't been tinkering with the car! Can you imagine having to chase it down the street?"

They ended up leaning against one another as they laughed long and hard.

Two beagles and three chihuahuas turned out to be a lot more difficult to handle than Ray imagined. The beagles stared up at him with droopy eyes as they sat on their haunches, unwilling to move. And the chihuahuas wouldn't hold still and kept trying to scurry forward, yapping at everything that moved.

On the sidewalk Ray kept pulling on the beagles'

leashes with his left hand, saying, "C'mon! Move! Walk!" At the same time, as the chihuahuas tried to run forward, he shouted at them, "Stop! Heel! Halt!"

He finally got the five of them to the park. The beagles moved slowly behind him, while the chihuahuas pulled their leashes taut ahead of him.

There was a family having a picnic in the park, a mother and father and two small children. They had food spread out over one of the park's many picnic tables . . . and they had a German shepherd.

As Ray and the five dogs passed the family's picnic table, the German shepherd trotted over, curious and grinning, pink tongue lolling.

The chihuahuas went berserk, yapping and hopping and dancing in circles. The beagles flopped to the ground lazily, lying there as if they never intended to move again.

Ray eyed the approaching German shepherd for a moment, then turned to the beagles and tugged on their leashes. "Hey!" he shouted. "C'mon, you guys, let's go! Move it, okay?"

As Ray was trying to get the beagles to move, the chihuahuas rushed toward the German shepherd, and before he knew it, Ray no longer had hold of their leashes. The chihuahuas had broken free.

"Oh, no!" Ray said, as he watched the chihua-huas race toward the German shepherd, yapping sharply all the way. He let go of the beagles' leashes and ran after the chihuahuas, shouting, "Hey! Stop! Heel!"

Ray imagined the chihuahuas being mangled by the large German shepherd, and he dreaded ex-plaining their deaths to the owners—and then hav-ing to explain it all to Robyn. He ran even faster, calling, "Come back! C'mon, come back! *Please!*"

But they didn't come back. They kept running toward the German shepherd, yapping wildly and viciously.

And the German shepherd froze in place for a moment, then turned and ran, yelping as if it were being attacked by a bear. As the big dog dove under the picnic table for cover, it pulled the table-cloth with it, and the family's picnic was scattered all over the ground.

By then, Ray was able to throw himself on the trailing leashes, bringing the chihuahuas to a yap-ping halt.

"I'm sorry!" Ray called to the family. They were so busy cleaning up the mess, they hardly noticed him at all.

Ray dragged the chihuahuas back to the edge of

the park. The weary-looking beagles were still lying lazily on the ground where he'd left them. They stared up at Ray as if he were the goofiest creature on the planet.

As happy as he was to be working, Ray could hardly wait for the day to finally be over.

CHAPTER 6

By the time he got home, Ray was exhausted. But he was still about twenty dollars short of his goal. He went to the refrigerator and got a soda, then flopped into a chair at the kitchen table.

Mr. Alvarado had left that morning to see Charlie, a mechanic friend of his; together, they were going to replace the car's faulty transmission. He had not returned yet, and Ray was alone. The silence in the house made his spirits sink even lower.

Ray decided what he needed most—besides another twenty dollars—was a long, hot shower. On his way to the bathroom, he passed the small desk where his dad handled all the bills. There on the desk was a white envelope with the name *Ray* written on it in block letters. Ray stopped and stared at the envelope for a moment, then picked it up and opened it.

Inside, he found six twenty-dollar bills! One hundred and twenty dollars!

Ray stared at the money, confused. He wondered if his dad had changed his mind. Maybe he'd decided to help Ray with some money after all. But one hundred and twenty dollars? Why so much?

Ray put the money back in the envelope and placed it on the desk again. It couldn't be for him, not that money. But why was his name written on the envelope?

He decided to think on it in the shower and, leaving the envelope of money on the desk, headed for the bathroom.

By the time he'd toweled off and dressed, Ray convinced himself it would probably be okay to take twenty from the envelope. That was all he needed. He wouldn't touch the rest, just in case it was there for some purpose he was unaware of. But with his name on the envelope, what could that purpose possibly be? If it turned out that his name on the envelope was a mistake and he was taking money he had no business taking, Ray would, of course, apologize to his dad and pay him back in no time at all.

Slipping a twenty-dollar bill from the envelope, he combined it with the rest of the money he had saved, and stuffed it all in his envelope. It was getting late, and St. Smythe's Magic Emporium would be closing soon. He grabbed his coat and hurried out of the house, eager to pay the entry fee that would make him an official member of the Young Magicians' Society.

"Ray, my boy!" Mr. St. Smythe said from behind the counter at the magic shop. "What brings you here this evening, just minutes before closing time?"

Ray smiled as he approached the counter, opening his wallet. "I've got the money for the entry fee, Mr. St. Smythe!" he said happily.

Mr. St. Smythe's smile disappeared and he stiffened suddenly, glancing around the store quickly. He came around the counter and put a hand on Ray's wrist to keep him from opening his wallet.

"Come with me, Ray," he said quietly. He took Ray's elbow and led him into the back room with the round table and the poster of Mr. St. Smythe in his youth. "All right, now," he said with a smile. "You say you have the entry fee?"

"Yes!" Ray said, beaming. He took the money from his wallet and handed it over to Mr. St. Smythe, with exactly ninety-five cents in change.

"That is simply *grand*, my boy!" Mr. St. Smythe said. "You're just in time, too. There were only two openings left this morning, and just this afternoon, a young man about your age paid his entry fee and took one of them. You have just filled the very *last* opening in the Young Magicians' Society, Ray. Welcome aboard."

Ray was so happy, he wanted to let out a shout, jump up, and shoot a victorious fist in the air. But he simply grinned at Mr. St. Smythe as he asked, "So, what do I do now?"

"I'll tell you precisely what you do now, my boy," Mr. St. Smythe said, folding the money and slipping it into his pocket. "You come back here tomorrow, and we'll begin your lessons in the magic arts."

Ray couldn't contain his excitement. He laughed out loud, then said, "Yes, sir! I'll be here!"

When he left the St. Smythe Magic Emporium, Ray was wearing a very large, triumphant grin. His hard work had paid off, and everything was going just perfectly.

* * *

Ray leaped out of his seat the instant the last bell of the day rang at school. He couldn't wait to begin his first lesson in the magic arts. He wasted no time getting out of the school building, not bothering to stop by his locker on the way.

When he finally walked into the St. Smythe Magic Emporium, Ray felt different than he had all the other times he'd gone into the store. He felt a strong sense of belonging, a sense of membership. He felt as if the store were, in a way, partly *his* store. He belonged there.

Mr. St. Smythe was not behind the counter when Ray walked in, so he decided to wait awhile, knowing the man would appear soon.

Fifteen minutes later, Mr. St. Smythe was still nowhere to be seen, so Ray approached one of the young men behind the counter. He was a red-haired guy in his early twenties whom Ray had seen performing magic tricks for customers on several occasions.

"Excuse me," Ray said with a smile. "I'm here to see Mr. St. Smythe."

The young man raised one eyebrow as he looked Ray over suspiciously. "I'm sorry," he said, "but Mr. St. Smythe isn't here right now."

"Do you know when he'll be back?" Ray asked.

"No. He didn't say. In fact, I don't even know

if he'll be back. So why don't you just run along and—"

Ray heard Mr. St. Smythe's British-accented voice and turned his head to the right just in time to see the man coming out of the back corridor of the store with Mr. Burke. Turning back to the red-haired guy behind the counter, Ray narrowed his eyes and said, "He isn't here right now, huh?"

The young man looked at the two men walking behind the counter. He coughed once, nervously, then hurried off.

Mustering a smile, Ray hurried down the counter to Mr. St. Smythe. "Well," he said happily, "I'm here for my first lesson."

Mr. St. Smythe stopped talking to Mr. Burke and stared down at Ray with a completely blank face. "I beg your pardon?" he said.

"My lesson, Mr. St. Smythe. Now that I'm a member of the Young Magicians' Society, I'm here for my first lesson in the magic arts."

Not only did Mr. St. Smythe not smile or respond in his usual friendly way, he stared at Ray without any sign of recognition. His blue-gray eyes looked coldly at Ray above the wire-rimmed glasses perched on his nose.

Ray's smile drained from his face. "Uh . . . Mr. St. Smythe?"

"Do I know you, my boy?" Mr. St. Smythe asked with a slight frown.

"Well, yeah, sure, Mr. St. Smythe, I've been coming in here for—"

"You certainly don't look familiar to me," Mr. St. Smythe interrupted. He turned to Mr. Burke. "Does this boy look familiar to you, Mr. Burke? I can't seem to place him."

Without blinking, or moving a muscle in his face, Mr. Burke silently shook his head back and forth.

"I didn't think so," Mr. St. Smythe said, scowling down at Ray again.

Ray's eyes widened as he frowned up at the silver-haired man. His mouth felt dry and his legs felt weak. "Uh, look, Mr. St. Smythe, I've been coming in here nearly every day for the last week, and you said if I paid the entry fee, I'd be a member of the Young Magicians' Society. And then you'd start teaching me the magic arts. That's what you *said!* A-and just last night, I came in here and I paid the seventy-nine dollars and ninety-five cents that you said would get me into the Young Magicians' Society. And you told me to come back today to start my lessons. So, here I am!"

Mr. St. Smythe folded his arms over his chest and frowned as he looked down at Ray. "I'm afraid you've made some kind of mistake, my boy.

I've never heard of such a thing as the Young—what did you call it? The Young Magicians' Club?"

"*Society!*" Ray snapped.

Mr. St. Smythe shook his head. "No, no. You've made a mistake. Perhaps you're thinking of some other magic store. There's no Young—"

"There *is* no other magic store in Paradise Valley!" Ray interrupted, raising his voice. "And it was *you*, Mr. St. Smythe! *You* were the one who promised to teach me the secrets of the magic arts. And now that I've given you my money, I want to start my lessons!" Ray's heartbeat was increasing, and his face felt hot.

Mr. St. Smythe pooched out his fat, pink lower lip as he shook his head very slowly. "You've given me no money, young man. Not a cent. And I promised you nothing, absolutely nothing. In fact, I've never met you before. Now, run along and don't cause trouble."

Ray's mouth dropped open wide as he stared up at Mr. St. Smythe in disbelief. It took him a moment to find his voice, but when he finally did, he shouted, "Are you *joking?* Is this some sort of trick?"

Mr. St. Smythe flinched and dropped his arms at his sides. "Young man, you're out of line, shouting at me like that. I insist that you leave this store now. Otherwise, I'll have you—"

"Mr. St. Smythe, you're *lying!*" Ray snapped. "I've been in here almost every day this past week, and just last night, I gave you nearly eighty dollars so I could be a member of the Young Magicians' Society. You ripped me off!"

"Look here, my boy," Mr. St. Smythe said firmly. "I have no idea *what* you're talking about. And I will *not* tolerate this kind of behavior in my store!" He turned to Mr. Burke and said, "Remove this young hooligan from the store immediately!" To Ray, he said, "And don't come back!"

Mr. Burke came around the counter and towered over Ray like a huge building of flesh and bone. Without speaking, he put an enormous hand on Ray's shoulder and turned him around. Gripping each of Ray's shoulders, Mr. Burke began pushing him toward the door.

"Wait," Ray said, "wait just a second!" He stepped forward, away from Mr. Burke's hands, and spun around. "You took money from me and—"

Mr. Burke clapped a hand over Ray's mouth suddenly. Closing his thumb and forefingers on Ray's cheeks, he pushed Ray backward, until they reached the door. Mr. Burke pulled the door open, then shoved Ray through it hard.

Ray stumbled backward, then fell on his backside. When he raised his head, the door had already banged shut.

Ray did not go straight home. He took a long walk after his humiliating and infuriating exile from the St. Smythe Magic Emporium. He didn't know what to do next. He'd worked so hard for the money to join the Young Magicians' Society, and he'd even taken some money that might not have been his to take. *I can't believe I gave that money to Mr. St. Smythe!* he said to himself. *How could I be so stupid?*

It was becoming obvious to Ray that the whole thing had been nothing more than a scam, a trick to get Ray to give Mr. St. Smythe eighty bucks. He had to decide what to do next, now that he knew the Young Magicians' Society was just a money-making trap.

He'd already told Alex about his plans to become a member of the society and learn from Mr. St. Smythe. She had not seemed very enthusiastic about it; although, like a true friend, she'd given him her support. Now that he knew the truth about the Young Magicians' Society, he wished he hadn't told her about it. If he went to her now and told her what had happened, he would look like a fool. He wouldn't blame her if she said "I told you so."

But he had to tell someone, he had to *do* something. If Mr. St. Smythe had done this to him, there was a good chance he was doing it to other kids.

Ray decided to talk to Alex. She was, after all, his best friend. And if she supported his *joining* the Young Magicians' Society, then she would most likely support him in *exposing* it. Ray was counting on her.

CHAPTER 7

"He's not a magician, he's a con man!" Alex exclaimed after Ray told her the whole story.

They were in Alex's bedroom, each sitting on the edge of one of the beds, facing one another.

Ray sighed heavily. "I should have known," he said, shaking his head. "You knew, didn't you? I mean, when I told you about it, you didn't seem really crazy about the idea."

"Well, eighty bucks is a lot of money for magic lessons, Ray."

"Hey, how was I supposed to know how much magic lessons cost? I mean, do *you* know the going rate for lessons in the magic arts from the greatest magician in all of Europe?"

"Yeah, I bet that's a bunch of garbage, too. More like the greatest rip-off artist in all of Europe!"

"I don't know," Ray said, shaking his head slowly. "He was pretty good at those tricks."

"But they're just props, Ray! All you have to do is pull a lever, or slip open a false bottom. That's how those things work. They're easy once you know the secret. There's no great mystery to it, and it doesn't take a lot of talent."

Ray's shoulders drooped. "Yeah, I guess I should've known. It just sounded like so much fun . . . being a magician and performing magic tricks for audiences . . . getting all that applause, making all that money. It would be like having my own special powers, like you do."

Alex went to his side, sat down, and put an arm around his shoulders. "I'm sorry, Ray. I shouldn't be snapping at you. I know how disappointed you are."

Ray shrugged.

"I was taken in by that Mr. St. Smythe guy, too," Alex added. "He was so nice, so . . . charming. And underneath all that charm, he was nothing but a lying, stealing rat!"

Nodding silently, Ray stared at the floor with a long face.

"What about that money you took from the envelope on your dad's desk?" Alex asked.

"I don't know. The envelope had my name on it, so I figured it was for me. And out of a hundred and twenty dollars, all I needed was twenty, so . . . I took it. But maybe I was wrong. Maybe the money was meant for something else."

"Has your dad mentioned it?"

"The envelope wasn't on the desk last night. He didn't say anything about it, but then, maybe he hasn't noticed there's a twenty-dollar bill missing yet."

"Did you say anything to him?"

Ray shook his head. "I'm afraid to now. I'm afraid I made a big mistake. Why didn't I wait and ask him first?" Ray asked himself, frustrated.

"You're going to have to bring it up sometime," Alex said softly.

"I know. I'm not looking forward to it, but"— Ray swallowed hard—"sooner or later, I've got to talk to him."

Alex stood and began to pace back and forth between the beds, frowning thoughtfully. "I wonder how many other kids Mr. St. Smythe has duped into joining the Young Magicians' Society."

"I don't know. I never heard him mention the society to anyone else."

"Maybe not," she said, tugging on her chin, "but I bet he mentioned it to plenty of people. Other customers just like you, Ray. Let's face it, seventy-nine ninety-five might be a lot of money to you and me, but it's not much to someone like Mr. St. Smythe. So, if he wants to make a lot of money, he's going to have to fool a bunch of other kids to join the Young Magicians' Society. And that means he's probably still at it."

"I can see the wheels turning in your head, Alex," Ray said suspiciously. "What are you thinking?"

Alex sat down across from Ray again and leaned forward. A clever smile was playing on her lips. "Remember how I said I'd 'conjure up something'? Well, I think I'm going to pay Mr. St. Smythe a visit tomorrow, after school. I helped you get into this mess, now I'm helping you get out."

"Hey, wait just a second," Ray said, his eyes widening. "I got myself into this. I don't want you getting into any trouble because of some stupid mistake I made!"

"Don't worry, Ray," she said. Her smile became a grin. "I won't get into any trouble."

Ray rolled his eyes and said, "Where have I heard that before? What are you going to do there?"

"Just look around. And listen. And don't worry, Mr. St. Smythe won't even know I'm there. *No* one will know. We're going to find out how many others Mr. St. Smythe is ripping off, and then we're gonna teach him a few lessons!"

Ray grinned.

"And, Ray," she said, "don't *ever* think you need special powers. Your special powers are . . . well, just being you!" she said with a laugh.

"Thanks, Alex."

"Now," Alex said, standing, "let's go make some popcorn. There's an old scary movie on TV in a few minutes."

"Which one?"

"The Mad Magician!"

They laughed together as they left the bedroom.

After school the next day, Alex and Ray walked for a while with Nicole, Robyn, and Louis. Then, as the two of them had planned the night before, Ray and Alex each made excuses for having to rush off, and they went their separate ways. They didn't want the others coming along, since Alex was planning to use her powers at the magic emporium and she couldn't be seen.

A few minutes later, just as they'd planned, Alex

and Ray met at an intersection in town and headed for the magic store.

"We should go to the back of the store," Alex said. "Remember, you've got to stay out of sight, Ray. If Mr. St. Smythe or his pet gorilla, Mr. Burke, sees you, they'll make trouble."

"You don't have to remind me," Ray said. "Believe me, Mr. Burke looks a lot bigger when he's coming at you like a Mack truck!"

A narrow, alleylike road ran behind the stores on the block where the St. Smythe Magic Emporium was located. The road was used by delivery trucks and the garbage collector. On that crisp Tuesday afternoon, it was also used by Alex and Ray.

They huddled beside a banged-up old garbage Dumpster and watched the back door of the magic store.

"Okay," Alex whispered, "I'll go in under the back door. Once I'm inside, I'll look around, see if I can learn anything about what Mr. St. Smythe is up to."

"Be careful," Ray warned.

"Yeah, I will. But if something *does* go wrong, you be ready to run, okay?"

Ray chuckled nervously. "Are you kidding? I'm ready to run now."

"Wait right here," Alex said. "I'll be back in a few minutes."

Ray took a deep breath and let it out slowly as he watched Alex walk casually to the back door of St. Smythe's Magic Emporium. He was sure there was no reason to be afraid. Mr. St. Smythe might be a liar and a thief, but surely he wouldn't actually *hurt* Alex if he were to catch her snooping around in his store.

Then again . . . Ray couldn't forget the scary sight of the enormous Mr. Burke filling his entire field of vision as he'd clamped down on Ray last night in the store, pushing him out onto the sidewalk.

As Ray watched, Alex stopped outside the door of the magic store and took a moment to concentrate. After a while, her body took on that shimmering, wobbly look that Ray could never quite get used to . . . and then she dissolved into a silvery puddle on the ground.

Ray crossed his fingers as Alex oozed through the narrow crack beneath the door and disappeared into the St. Smythe Magic Emporium.

Inside the store, Alex flowed over the floor in a puddle. She tried to move quickly, but at the same time carefully. She didn't have much time, but she didn't want to attract attention, either. As she oozed, she carefully watched and listened.

As usual, there were at least a dozen customers browsing around in the large store, young and old alike. None of them appeared to be seriously interested in the merchandise, though; they were simply there out of curiosity, checking out the new store in town, seeing what it had to offer.

Alex spotted two boys at the counter, near the cash register. One was chubby with blond hair, the other thin with black hair and braces on his teeth. They were each about ten or eleven years old. They were speaking rather intensely with a shifty-eyed, redheaded young man, one of the employees. Alex remembered seeing the redheaded guy performing magic tricks for the customers at the grand opening. She rippled toward the two boys and listened carefully.

As Alex approached them, the blond boy handed something to the redheaded guy and said, "Okay, there it is. Does that mean we're members of the Young Magicians' Society now?"

Alex saw that the boy had handed the redheaded guy a rolled-up wad of cash!

The redhead chuckled as he stuffed the money into his shirt pocket. "No, no, no," he said, "you misunderstood, David. To become a member of the

71

Young Magicians' Society, it costs fifty dollars *each*. Per *person*."

The boys looked at one another, eyes wide with shock.

The blond-haired boy said, "B-b-but that's a hundred dollars!"

"For both of you, yes," the redhead said with a nod. "Now, this money is just for *you*, right?" he asked the blond boy.

"Well, yeah." The boy looked at his friend rather sadly.

It was obvious to Alex that he'd been under the impression the fifty dollars would get both of them into the society, and he didn't want to leave his friend out.

But why fifty dollars? Alex wondered. For Ray, the fee had been seventy-nine dollars and ninety-five cents. She turned that over in her mind as she continued to observe the two boys.

"Don't worry, Eric," the redhead said to the black-haired boy. "You can join, too. But you'll need fifty dollars. And you'd better get it soon. By tomorrow, I'd say. Openings have been filling up very fast, and there's only one left. It won't be available for long."

"Okay," Eric said. "I'll go home and get it. I can be back in twenty minutes."

David looked at his friend with surprise, then turned to the redhead and said, "Uh, 'scuse us a second." He took Eric's arm and the two of them walked about six feet away from the counter and spoke in whispers. "What're you gonna do, Eric?"

"The same thing you did," Eric hissed. "I'm gonna *steal* it! You took the fifty bucks from your dad. Well, my brother's got twenty dollars hidden in his bookcase, and I know where my mom keeps some money tucked away. I'll go get it, come back here and pay him, then we'll *both* be members of the society, okay?"

Alex had to resist the urge to cry out, *No! Don't do it! They're ripping you off!* She remained silent.

"Well . . . okay," David said hesitantly. "Just don't get caught."

"Did you get caught? No! So, neither will I!"

They returned to the redheaded guy behind the counter, and Eric said, "I'll be back with the money in just a little while. Can you hold that opening for me?"

"Oh, no, I'm sorry," the redhead said with a smug smile. "That's against policy. You'd better hurry."

As the boys rushed out of the store together, the redhead took the cash from his coat pocket and began to count it. Alex was so angry at him that she wanted to give him a good swift kick in the shin. But she didn't have a foot at the moment, so she oozed away from him to a corner of the store.

There, another employee was performing a trick for a girl. The employee was a man in his twenties, tall and slender, with a silver-capped tooth in the front of his mouth that flashed whenever he smiled.

The girl was Alex's age, pretty, with long auburn hair. Alex didn't recognize her, but she was wearing a private school uniform, so she attended a different school.

The girl watched in awe as the silver-toothed guy made a silver ball float behind a silk scarf he held up between both hands. It floated above the scarf, then below the scarf. It hovered between his hands with the scarf draped over it. Then, when he jerked the scarf away, the silver ball was gone!

"Unbelievable!" the girl exclaimed, grinning. "How did you do that?"

"Oh, no," the silver-toothed guy said with a smirk, tucking the scarf away in a pocket. "I can't tell you that. The first rule of magic is that you never tell your secrets to anyone . . . except another professional magician."

Alex remembered Mr. St. Smythe giving the same line to Ray on the day of the grand opening.

The silver-toothed guy leaned toward the girl and said, "However, if you'd really like to learn how to do this sort of thing, there's a group you could join. And if you're really serious about it"—he reached out and appeared to pull a dollar bill out of the girl's ear—"you can make a lot of these. Here, keep it." He handed the dollar bill to the girl. "After all, it came out of your ear!"

Mr. St. Smythe pulled the same trick on Ray! Alex thought. *Everybody in the store is in on this scam!*

"Really?" the girl asked as she took the dollar bill. Her voice was whispery and filled with awe. "What group is that?"

"The Young Magicians' Society," the silver-toothed guy said. "You'd be able to take lessons in the magic arts from Mr. St. Smythe, the owner of the store. He was once considered the greatest magician in all of Europe."

Oh, brother! Alex thought. She didn't want to stick around for any more of the silver-toothed guy's spiel—she'd heard it already from Ray. But as she oozed away from them, she hoped the girl wouldn't fall for the lie.

Alex rushed over the floor, staying out of sight, behind counters, beneath display cases. She didn't see Mr. St. Smythe anywhere in the store and assumed he was in the back room Ray had told her about, the room in which he'd shown Ray the poster of himself as a younger man.

Ray had given her detailed directions to that room, and she followed them carefully, oozing to the back of the store, then to the left, down the corridor, and into the room. She squirmed as she moved over the cold, dirty, concrete floor, careful to ooze around the cigarette and cigar butts.

Mr. St. Smythe was there with a blond boy Alex recognized from school, Norman Sweeney, who had three books tucked under his left arm. Alex didn't know Norman well, but she'd seen him around, and she knew Ray sometimes hung out with him. The hulking Mr. Burke was there, too, seated at a table, smoking a cigar and playing with a deck of cards.

Alex quickly snaked her way under the table and stayed there as she watched Mr. St. Smythe and Norman. They were several feet away, and the white-haired man was showing Norman something on the wall. Alex watched and listened intently.

"I was, for a time, considered the greatest magician in all of Europe," Mr. St. Smythe said. "But that was when I wore a younger man's clothes, Norman. Today, I am content to pass my knowledge on to young people like you, to keep alive the secrets of the magic arts."

"I don't know if I could ever be a magician," Norman said. "It looks like it takes a lot of discipline. You probably have to spend every spare minute practicing, don't you? I mean, to be that good?"

Mr. St. Smythe smiled and said, "My boy, you can be anything you want to be, and if you want to be a practitioner of the magic arts, then that is what you should be. And as for discipline and hard work—anything that can be attained without those simply isn't worth having."

"How do I join?"

"With a simple entry fee of ninety-nine ninety-five," Mr. St. Smythe said, "you may begin your lessons."

Ninety-nine ninety-five? Alex thought. *The price has changed again? What's going on here?*

Alex knew that Norman's parents were both doctors and money wasn't a problem in their family. Could Mr. St. Smythe also know that somehow? Maybe Norman had mentioned it earlier in their conversation. Maybe *that's* why the prices varied from person to person, Alex figured. Apparently Mr. St. Smythe and his henchmen changed the price according to how much money they thought each young customer could come up with in a few days or so.

After thinking about it for a long moment, Norman said, "Ninety-nine ninety-five, huh? Could I make payments?"

"I'm afraid it's not my policy to take payments," Mr. St. Smythe said. "But do not misunderstand me. I am *not* trying to pressure you. If you have the money, fine. If you don't, that is fine, too. Perhaps later, when you can afford it, you can join— if there are any openings left."

"Any openings left?" Norman asked. "What do you mean?"

"Well, I can only take on a limited number of students at a time," Mr. St. Smythe said. "As you know, we're new here in Paradise Valley, but the Young Magicians' Society tends to fill up rather quickly."

Norman frowned and chewed his lower lip for a moment. "Well, in that case, Mr. St. Smythe, I could get the money today. I've got some saved up—not quite enough, but I could probably get the rest from my parents."

"Wonderful, Norman! I'm happy to hear it." He smiled down at Norman. "But if I were you, I'd be sure to do it today. I wouldn't want you to miss out."

The puddle that was Alex rippled with anger beneath the table. And then she caught a whiff of cigar smoke. It pushed her closer and closer to coughing. But she resisted, summoning all her strength to keep quiet and undetected . . . until Mr. Burke threw the fat, brown, ugly cigar butt beneath the table to the already dirty concrete floor. But it didn't land on the concrete floor. . . . It landed on Alex with an ugly sizzling sound!

Letting loose a sharp yelp, Alex rose up from the puddle on the floor and regained her natural form. Her head bumped the underside of the table-top hard, nearly knocking it over. She crouched down, holding her breath in fear. Maybe no one noticed?

But Mr. Burke pushed his chair back suddenly and stood. He moved the table to one side with a noisy scraping sound and glared down at Alex, his meaty fists clenched.

CHAPTER 8

Norman was so startled by the sudden commotion that he dropped his books and they scattered over the floor. As he hunkered down to retrieve them, Mr. St. Smythe barked, "What is the meaning of this?" Mr. St. Smythe's unctuous smile was replaced by a scowl. "Who are you? Why were you hiding under that table?" he demanded.

Standing slowly, Alex said nothing. Her eyes darted back and forth between Mr. St. Smythe and Mr. Burke, glancing now and then at Norman. Her head spun as she tried to think of something reasonable to say.

Norman stood, looking confused, his books under his arm again. Mr. St. Smythe quickly pushed him toward the door, saying, "Excuse me, but I'm afraid we'll have to continue our conversation later. Run along now. Why don't you go get your money? I'll see you later, my boy."

Mr. St. Smythe slammed the door, then turned to Alex again. "Well? Who are you? And what are you up to?"

Alex could think of nothing to say . . . so she ran!

"Go after her!" Mr. St. Smythe barked at Mr. Burke. "Find out if she knows anything!"

Alex heard Mr. Burke moving toward her as she fumbled with the doorknob. She finally got the door open, bolted from the room, and ran down the corridor.

Outside, Ray paced beside the Dumpster, anxiously waiting for some sign of Alex. He checked his watch for the sixth time. She'd been in the store about five minutes already. He wondered if it was going well . . . if she was coming across any useful information they could use against Mr. St. Smythe . . . or if she'd been caught by the old man or any of his flunkies. Ray's palms were sweaty, and he realized he was occasionally muttering to himself like a crazy person.

The magic store's back door suddenly burst open

and Alex raced out into the alley, running as fast as she could! The door swung closed behind her.

"Run!" she shouted.

Ray froze, unable to move for a moment as Alex ran toward him. He saw the door open again and gulped when he spotted Mr. Burke bounding after Alex.

"C'mon, Ray!" Alex shouted. "Run!"

Together, they hurried down the alley. Behind them, they could hear Mr. Burke's shoes clomping heavily on the pavement as he ran after them. And he was rapidly closing the distance between them! Ray was amazed by how quickly the enormous man could move. His size did not seem to be slowing him down in the least.

Ray and Alex ran down the alley, and finally, into the side street to which it was connected. A horn honked, and there was a shrill squeal of brakes. Ray's heart skipped a beat when he looked to the right and saw a blue Chevy Blazer jerk to a stop just a few feet before running them down.

Ray and Alex froze in place for a moment, staring at one another with bulging eyes. They'd almost been killed!

The driver of the Blazer stuck his head out the window and shouted, "Hey! Why don't you look before you cross! Crazy kids!" He drove around them and went on down the road.

Ray and Alex looked behind them. Mr. Burke was closing on them quickly!

They crossed the street and ran into the alley that continued down the next block behind another row of shops. They passed more garbage Dumpsters and dodged a stray cat as it crossed the alley, giving them a puzzled stare.

They had almost reached the end of the alley and come to the next street when Ray glanced back over his shoulder.

Mr. Burke was gone!

"Hey, Alex!" Ray called. They stopped.

Alex was gasping for breath. Morphing took a lot of energy, and she looked exhausted. "Where'd he go?" she asked.

"I don't know, but this looks too easy. Why would he just give up on us?"

"What should we do? Keep heading in the direction we were going, or turn back?"

"I'm not sure. Do you think he'd quit chasing us that easily?" Ray asked.

"Let's hope so." Alex took Ray's elbow. "C'mon, let's just keep going this way."

They walked warily, each of them glancing backward now and then until they reached the end of the alley. Before they could peer around the corner of the last building, Mr. Burke appeared in front of them! Alex and Ray turned to run back into the alley again, but the bulky goon grabbed Alex's shoulders and held her back.

"Ray!" Alex cried.

Ray stopped and spun around. When he saw Mr. Burke holding Alex back, he felt a rush of panic.

Alex struggled for a moment, then stopped moving. An instant later, Mr. Burke stumbled backward against the sudden invisible force of Alex's force field. The moment he released her, Alex ran away from him and caught up with Ray.

"C'mon!" Alex shouted as she began to run.

By the time they reached the end of the alley, Ray spotted Mr. St. Smythe standing across the street. The man eyed Ray angrily, pointed a finger at him and said, "You! I thought I told you to stay away from my store!"

Ray and Alex turned right and raced along the sidewalk. They knew Mr. St. Smythe wasn't going to come running after them. But still, they didn't stop running till they got to the park.

Inside the park grounds, Alex lay down on top of a picnic table to catch her breath. Ray sat on the bench, doubled over and panting. When he realized it was the same picnic table under which the chihuahuas had chased the German shepherd, he laughed wearily.

"What's so funny?" Alex asked.

"The other day I ruined a family's picnic lunch at this table," Ray said. "And I was just thinking, I was so scared back there, while Mr. Burke was chasing us, that I almost lost *my* lunch!"

Alex laughed. "Yeah, me too. Boy oh boy, I could use a long nap."

"So, did you learn anything useful while you were sneaking around inside the store?" Ray asked.

"Well, for one thing, you're definitely not the only one Mr. St. Smythe has weaseled some money out of. And Mr. St. Smythe isn't the only one in the store doing it. From what I could tell, *all* the employees are in on it!"

She told him about the redheaded guy behind the counter, and the silver-toothed guy, and how Mr. St. Smythe told Norman Sweeney about the Young Magicians' Society.

"They got Norm Sweeney?" Ray asked, frowning.

"I don't know if they *got* him, but Mr. St. Smythe was sure dangling the bait. What bothered me the most were these two boys talking to the red-headed guy at the counter. One had stolen money from his dad, and the other left to steal it from his brother and mom. Can you *believe* that?"

Alex then told him about the different prices quoted to each customer. "It looks as though they're going after whatever they think they can get," she explained. "They knew those two kids would have a hard time getting hold of eighty dollars, so they dropped it to fifty apiece. But Mr. St. Smythe asked Norman for ninety-nine bucks, probably because he knows Norman's parents are both doctors. They go for whatever they think they can get out of the kids. And they don't care how the kids get the money, either. Even if they have to *steal* it!"

Ray released a long, heavy sigh. "Like I did," he said.

"You still haven't talked to your dad about that money?" Alex asked.

"No, and I've got a sick feeling in the pit of my stomach. And the pit of my stomach never lies. It always knows when I've done something wrong."

"Well, if that's the case, you'll just have to apologize to your dad," Alex said.

"But how can I pay him back?"

"Oh, that shouldn't be a problem." Alex smiled with satisfaction. "We're going to get your money back from Mr. St. Smythe."

"We are? How?"

Alex laughed. "I'm conjuring something up again. It's too late to do it today, so we'll have to wait until after school tomorrow. We'll do it first thing."

"Do what? Go to the police?"

"Nope. We won't have to do that. Because I'm gonna make Mr. St. Smythe call the police on *himself!*" Alex grinned, but she wouldn't tell Ray what she had in mind.

CHAPTER 9

During lunch at school the next day, Alex did not join her friends as she usually did. Instead, she went to the cafeteria, lunch bag in hand, looking for someone else, someone she hardly knew at all.

The night before, Alex had gone over and over her plan, and she'd realized that it was missing something. As she'd told Ray, she planned to make Mr. St. Smythe call the police on himself. When they arrived, she planned to have Ray there at the St. Smythe Magic Emporium to tell the police his story. But it would *still* be Ray's word against Mr. St. Smythe's. Even after Alex was finished with Mr. St. Smythe, there *still* would be no guarantee that the police would believe everything Ray told them.

Just to be safe, Alex decided they would need someone else there, someone who could talk to the police with Ray—another victim of Mr. St. Smythe's to back up the story.

While she'd been in the magic store yesterday in her liquefied form, Norman Sweeney had been the only person she'd recognized. She did not know, however, if Norman had fallen for Mr. St. Smythe's bait and joined the Young Magicians' Society. If he had, he might be able to back up Ray's story to the police. If not . . . well, maybe she could manage to somehow track down those two young boys she'd overheard talking about stealing the money they needed to join the society.

Alex spotted Norman at a table by one of the windows. He was with two other guys, but by the time Alex reached the table, they were standing to leave.

"Hi, Norman," she said with a smile as his two friends walked away with their trays.

Norman was blond and freckled and he wore large, wire-rimmed glasses. He looked startled when he looked up at Alex.

"Yeah?" he said, perplexed.

"I'm Alex Mack. We use the same study carrel in the library. You're usually finishing up when I get there to study."

"Oh, yeah, sure." He smiled uncertainly. "Hi, Alex."

"Mind if I sit with you?"

"Go ahead."

Alex sat down, opened her bag, and removed her sandwich, apple, and celery sticks. "Didn't I see you go into the St. Smythe Magic Emporium yesterday, Norman?" she asked.

"Yeah, I was there. But I didn't see you. Were you—"

"So, you're into magic, huh?" Alex interrupted Norman before he associated her with the commotion in the back room.

"Well, not really. I used to be when I was a little kid. My parents bought me a magic kit with some trick balls and cups and playing cards. I played with it a lot, but never stuck with it."

There was a silent moment as they ate, until Alex asked, "What did you think of the magic store?"

"It was cool!" Norman said, his eyes growing wide. "They've got really professional stuff in there. And the owner, Mr. St. Smythe, used to be a way famous magician once, in Europe."

"Did you buy anything?"

"Well, uh . . ." He munched on a potato chip thoughtfully. "I didn't exactly buy any . . . thing," he replied.

Alex frowned. "What do you mean?"

"I didn't buy any of the tricks or equipment they were selling. I was thinking about buying one of the how-to books on magic, but then Mr. St. Smythe told me about something called the Young Magicians' Society."

Alex listened as Norman told her all about the Young Magicians' Society. Then she asked, "Did you join?"

Grinning, Norman nodded eagerly. "Yep. I'd saved up nearly ninety dollars to buy a modem for my computer so I could get on the Net. But my parents gave me one for my birthday a few months ago. So the money was just sitting there. . . ." He shrugged with one shoulder as his words trailed off.

"How much did it cost to join?" Alex asked.

"Well, I figured it was gonna be really expensive, like maybe two or three hundred dollars, you know? But it was only a hundred bucks. I know that's a lot of money, but I had the ninety dollars in my bank account and I borrowed the rest from my parents."

"Did you tell them what the money was for?"

"No. It was just ten bucks and change. They didn't ask."

"When do you start your lessons?"

"Today," Norman said happily.

He kept talking, but Alex tuned him out for a few moments as her mind raced frantically. She knew that when Norman returned to the St. Smythe Magic Emporium for his first lesson, there would be no such thing as the Young Magicians' Society. She knew he would be kicked out of the store and told never to return, and he would *not* get his ninety-nine dollars and ninety-five cents back.

But should she tell him that was going to happen? Should she warn him? Wasn't it kind of a cruel hoax *not* to tell him?

Well, maybe not, Alex thought. *He's already given them the money, and telling him what I know might be telling him too much.*

Alex feared that telling Norman could make him suspicious of her upcoming performance in the store. If he didn't believe her, it could even spoil her plan altogether! She decided to tell him nothing about her or Ray's experiences with Mr. St. Smythe and Mr. Burke. But she wanted to make sure Norman was in the St. Smythe Magic Emporium at the right time.

In fact, now that Norman was going to be unwittingly involved in her plan, the whole thing was going to have to be carefully timed, right down to the second.

". . . so, anyway," Norman was saying, "I'm going in right after school. I think this is gonna be fun, taking magic lessons from one of the greatest magicians in Europe."

"Are you going right after school?" Alex asked. "As in, immediately?"

"Uh-huh." He grinned. "I'm psyched to get started with the lessons right away."

If Norman went straight from school to the St. Smythe Magic Emporium, he would be kicked out of the store before she and Ray could get there. Alex wondered how she could stall him, just for a little while.

"You know, if you show up a little later, you can meet Ray there," she said, hoping it would work.

"Really?" Norman asked. "How much later?"

Alex took a big bite of her sandwich to give herself a moment to think. She knew Norman was excited about starting the magic lessons he thought he'd be getting, so she knew he wouldn't wait *too* long. But she and Ray would need time to prepare and put her plan into action.

"Oh, I don't know," Alex said with a casual shrug. "Maybe . . . till four-thirty?"

Norman smiled again as he asked, "Will you be there, too, Alex?"

Hmm, Alex thought. *I don't want to lead him on, but he's a nice guy, so I don't want to scare him off, either.*

"I don't know," she said. "I might. It depends. I've got some things to do after school. If I can get everything done in time, I'll be there. But even if I'm not, I think you should meet Ray there. He's interested in magic, too, you know."

"Really?"

"Oh, yeah. He went to the St. Smythe Magic Emporium on the day of the grand opening."

"I didn't know Ray was into magic, too." Norman finished his lunch, thinking it over. "Okay. I guess I can wait a little longer. It'd be more fun with Ray there, anyway. Hey, maybe I can get him into the Young Magicians' Society. I bet he'd love to join."

Oh, if you only knew, Alex thought. Then she said, "I'll tell him to look for you."

"Great!"

Alex stuffed all her lunch wrappings into the brown bag. "Thanks for sharing your table with me, Norman," she said, smiling as she stood.

"No problem." Norman nodded toward her

wadded-up paper bag. "I can throw that away for you. Just put it on the tray."

"Thanks." She dropped the bag onto his lunch tray. "I'll see you around, okay?"

"Sure, Alex. Nice talking to you."

Nicole and Robyn were waiting for Alex at the cafeteria door. They fell into step with her, one on each side.

"So, what's *this?*" Nicole said playfully. "Doing lunch with Norman?"

"Yeah!" Robyn added. "Some secret crush you haven't told us about?"

Alex laughed. "No. I was just having lunch with him, that's all."

"Uh-huh," Nicole prodded. "Norman Sweeney, huh? I didn't think he was your type, Alex."

"You never said a word about him to us," Robyn said.

"Would you guys stop it!" Alex said, still laughing. "Give me a break. I just sat at a table with him. He's a nice guy. And besides, I needed to ask him a couple of questions about something, that's all."

"You asked him *out?*" Robyn gasped.

"No!"

"What'd you have to ask him about, then?" Nicole asked.

Uh-oh, Alex thought. *What do I tell them?*

She decided to tell them the truth.

"I asked him about a club he joined at that new magic shop in town," she said as casually as she could.

"Oh? Thinking about becoming a magician?" Robyn asked.

"Oh, yeah, sure am," Alex said sarcastically. "So be careful . . . I just might saw you in half!"

The girls headed for their next class, laughing happily.

CHAPTER 10

When the last bell finally rang, Alex and Ray met in front of the school, just as they had agreed that morning. A large satchel hung from Alex's shoulder by a long leather strap. Ray gave the satchel a curious glance, because he'd never seen Alex carrying it before.

"So, what's your plan?" Ray asked.

"Well, for one thing, we don't have much time, so we're gonna have to hurry. First stop is the Re-Run Thrift Store," Alex replied.

Ray's eyebrows rose. "Really? For what, used clothes?"

"Yep. We're going there to find my costume," she said with a sly smile. "My mom has about seventy dollars in credit there, because that's where she takes a lot of our old stuff. It's a charity store, you know. All the money from their sales goes to the American Cancer Society."

Her costume? Ray thought. He had been so preoccupied with raising money to join the Young Magicians' Society, he'd nearly forgotten that Halloween was just around the corner. He assumed Alex was referring to a Halloween costume. As they walked away from school, Ray wondered what a costume had to do with the Young Magicians' Society. When he asked about her "plan," he'd meant her plan to deal with Mr. St. Smythe and Mr. Burke, not her plans for Halloween!

"Okay," Ray said. "And when we're done at Re-Run, then what?"

"Then we go through with the rest of my plan."

"The rest of your plan? You mean this costume is part of your plan? You're not getting ready for Halloween?"

Alex laughed. "No, silly, it's not for Halloween. It's for Mr. St. Smythe. After what happened yesterday, I couldn't just walk into the magic emporium as myself, could I?"

"No, I guess not."

"Besides," Alex continued, "even if Mr. St. Smythe and Mr. Burke had never seen me before, it wouldn't be a good idea to do what I'm going to do without a costume."

"And what are you going to do?"

"You'll see," she said with that same sly smile.

"Hey, cut it out!" Ray said, laughing as he poked her with an elbow. "Why are you keeping secrets?"

"Don't you want to be surprised?" Alex asked with a mischievous grin. "I mean, if I tell you everything, it'll spoil the fun!"

Ray rolled his eyes. "Alex, I've had enough surprises in the last few days to last me a long time. I don't need any more. Just give me some idea of what I'm getting into here, okay?"

"Well, you don't have to do much of anything. I'll do it all. You just have to wait outside the magic emporium for Norman Sweeney."

"What? Norm Sweeney is coming? How does he know to meet me outside the magic store?"

"I've already set that up. I talked to him at school today." Alex told Ray all about her lunch with Norman Sweeney. She explained that Norman had fallen for the Young Magicians' Society, just like Ray had, and was supposed to get his first lesson that very afternoon.

"So they *did* get Norm Sweeney," Ray said, frowning.

"They got him, all right. But Norman has to know they've ripped him off before he can help us. That's why this whole thing has to be timed just perfectly!"

"Oh? And how do we do that?" Ray asked.

As they continued walking, Alex explained to Ray exactly how her plan would have to be timed. In doing so, she told him the entire plan. As he listened, Ray's eyes widened; he wasn't so sure he liked the sound of it all.

By the time she was finished explaining the plan, Ray wondered if it could possibly work . . . and if he wanted to be there if it failed. In any case, he knew that if they weren't careful, it was going to be the kind of thing that would make the paper—and probably the front page! If *that* happened, and if Alex's identity was revealed, the secret of her powers would become common knowledge, which meant the people at the Paradise Valley Chemical plant would know about it. And that meant serious trouble.

But in spite of all those possibilities, Ray did not protest. He knew Alex very well, and he knew that once she'd made up her mind, there was no un-making it. He also knew that anything she set her mind to was usually a success. So, he went along with her plan to foil Mr. St. Smythe.

When they entered the Re-Run Thrift Store, they were greeted almost immediately by Nicole and Robyn.

"What're you guys doin' here?" Nicole asked.

"Hey, we could ask the same thing of you," Ray said, stalling for time as he tried to think of a plausible excuse for why they were at the thrift store.

"We're looking for Halloween costumes," Robyn said halfheartedly. "But I want to go as a human being. Have you noticed how rare human beings are lately? I mean, have you watched TV? Gone to the movies? Nothing but space aliens, everywhere you look. TV, movies . . . they're all space aliens. I'd like to go as a human being, but Nicole says I should get a costume."

Ray had no idea how he and Alex were going to explain their presence at the thrift store to Nicole and Robyn, but Alex solved the problem for him.

"I'm here looking for a costume, too," she said with a smile.

"I'm thinking something zombielike for me," Nicole said. "I told Robyn she should go as a vampire, 'cause she's so pale." She nudged Robyn with an elbow.

"Okay, so I'm pale, so sue me!" Robyn said. "But do you have any idea how dangerous sunbathing is these days? Tans are deadly! We're running out of ozone layer, so all those killer ultra-violet rays are—"

"That's enough, doom-girl," Alex said.

"So, what kind of costume are you looking for, Alex?" Nicole asked.

"Oh, something gypsy-ish," Alex said casually. "You know, a big flowing skirt, a few shawls, lots of jewelry. That sort of thing."

"Great!" Nicole said. "Let's go look together."

The girls disappeared among the racks of sec-ondhand clothes, laughing and chattering, leaving Ray alone. "Okay, fine," Ray muttered to himself with a shrug.

As the girls wandered through the store, brows-ing through the clothes and jewelry, Ray wandered around the store by himself, checking out the used CDs, videotapes, comic books, and paperbacks. He wasn't looking for anything in particular, just try-ing to kill time while the girls shopped. But when he started looking through some of the clothes . . .

. . . he found something that made him gasp. He stared down at it with wide eyes for a long mo-ment, then took it to the front counter.

When Alex was finished about fifteen minutes later, she left the store with a bag of clothes. Nicole and Robyn were still shopping inside. Ray was waiting just outside the door with a bag of his own.

"Oh, did you buy something, too?" Alex asked. "You know, you don't have to wear a costume."

"No, it's not a costume," Ray said as they began walking. "Just something I found."

"Okay, let's get to the Stop-n-Rob," Alex said, quickening her pace. "We don't have much time!"

One block behind the St. Smythe Magic Emporium, there was a combination gas station and convenience store. The sign rotating in slow circles above the gas islands read Stop-n-Run, but everybody called it the Stop-n-Rob because the little store's prices were so high.

There were rest rooms at the rear of the building. Alex ducked into the women's room. Seconds after the door closed behind her, it opened again and she poked her head out. "You'd better get out of here," she said to Ray. "Once I get this costume on, we shouldn't be seen together. Wait out front for Norman and tell him exactly what we agreed on. Then, at exactly four-fifteen, step inside the store."

"Okay," Ray said, somewhat nervously. "Um . . . shouldn't we synchronize our watches, or something?"

"Ray, you're not wearing a watch."

He glanced at his wrist. "Oh, yeah, guess I'm not."

"Just keep checking the clock outside the bank across the street, okay?"

He nodded. "Yeah, okay. Well, uh . . . good luck, Alex."

"Thanks," she said with a smile. "Now, beat it or you'll blow my cover!" She disappeared behind the bathroom door.

Ray made his way up the block to the St. Smythe Magic Emporium, hoping Alex's plan would work . . . or that, at the very least, it would not get one or both of them into big trouble.

Norman showed up at five minutes after four. "Hi, Ray," he said with a friendly smile.

"Hey, Norm, how's it going?" Ray said.

"Great! I'm here for my first magic lesson," Norm said, so excited that his eyebrows rose high above his glasses.

"Sounds good, Norm," Ray said, glancing around nervously for any sign of trouble. He didn't know what kind of trouble that might be, but he figured it was a good idea to keep an eye out for it.

"I didn't know you were into magic, Ray."

"Oh, yeah, Alex told you, huh? Well, I guess checking out this store is what really did it. That pushed me over the edge and all of a sudden, I was . . . into magic!"

"Well, let's go inside." Norman stepped forward and pushed the door open.

"Uh, tell you what," Ray said. "I'm gonna wait here for Alex. If she doesn't get here in a few minutes, I'll join you, okay?"

"Okay, sure. If you can't find me, just wait around a little while. I'll be in the back room taking my first lesson." He went into the store.

Ray was supposed to go into the store at four-fifteen, because that was when Alex was going to enter from the back. He and Alex had decided that if he went in sooner and waited for her to arrive, someone might recognize him from his last visit to the St. Smythe Magic Emporium and kick him out. She assured him that, once she got started, Mr. St. Smythe and his employees wouldn't notice him, because they'd be too busy paying attention to her.

He looked across the street at the big digital clock in front of the bank. Just five more minutes to go. Ray blew a long, anxious breath as he wondered how Alex was doing.

Alex collapsed into a liquefied puddle and oozed beneath the back door of the St. Smythe Magic Emporium, just as she had the day before. She made her way carefully over the floor, concealing herself beneath shelves and showcases whenever possible.

She planned to take her natural form and appear suddenly in the store—but it wouldn't exactly be her, Alex. It would, instead, be a taller, older woman, a mysterious-looking gypsy woman. In the rest room behind the Stop-n-Rob, Alex had transformed herself with a wig of thick, long, black hair, a lot of makeup, high heels to make her taller, and the shawls and gawdy jewelry she'd bought at the thrift store. She wore one of the shawls over her head like a hood, partially concealing her face.

Norman was at the counter talking to the long-haired, silver-toothed employee Alex had observed secretly the day before.

"I *told* you kid," Silver-tooth was saying, "I don't know what you're talking about."

"But I was just here yesterday!" Norman insisted. "I-I-I gave him almost a hundred dollars."

"Sorry, kid, but you're making a mistake. We don't sell magic lessons here. You see any signs advertising magic lessons? No. So why don't you just get lost, okay?"

Mr. St. Smythe came from the back of the store and joined the long-haired employee behind the counter. "Is there a problem, Mr. Jackson?" Mr. St. Smythe asked the guy.

"Just some kid giving me a hard time about magic lessons," Mr. Jackson said.

Mr. St. Smythe leaned forward and scowled down at Norman. "We do not teach magic lessons here, young man. Now run along and don't make trouble."

Norman stared up at the man and tried to speak, but he was so stunned, his lips just moved silently.

Alex looked at the clock on the wall, then at the glass door in the front of the store. She could see Ray stepping up to the door and pushing it open.

It was time.

CHAPTER 11

The instant Ray entered the St. Smythe Magic Emporium, a tall Gypsy woman appeared to grow up out of the floor just a few feet from the front counter. The big, dangling earrings and long necklaces she wore clanked and clattered loudly, getting Mr. St. Smythe's attention immediately. Mr. St. Smythe was so startled, he jerked upright and stood rigidly behind the counter, gawking at the Gypsy woman.

Ray clapped a hand over his mouth to hide his gasp. He was amazed at how different Alex looked! Of course, he knew her so well that he didn't think any costume could ever fool him—and it probably wouldn't fool Nicole and Robyn, either. But Ray suddenly knew it was going to work on everyone else in the store. He was sure even Norman, who saw her around school every day, would never suspect her true identity. She was completely transformed by her costume!

Alex raised her right arm slowly, her wrist clinking with dangly bracelets, and pointed at Mr. St. Smythe. She wore long false fingernails painted a deep blood red, and flashy multicolored rings on all her fingers. "Give that boy his money back, Mr. St. Smythe!" Alex said in a deep, throaty voice she'd been practicing since the previous night.

Mr. St. Smythe glared at Alex. "This is none of your concern, and I will thank you to be on your way and—"

"I'm *making* it my concern," Alex said, raising her voice a bit.

Others in the store, people who had not seen her appear out of nowhere, began to look toward the counter to see what all the fuss was about. Norman's back had been turned when Alex appeared. Only Mr. St. Smythe, the silver-toothed Mr. Jackson, and Ray had caught the Gypsy woman's magical entrance.

"And who, may I ask, are *you?*" Mr. St. Smythe snapped impatiently.

Alex took a step toward him and said quietly

and ominously, "I am the one who is going to give you a few lessons in the magic arts, Mr. St. Smythe."

Mr. St. Smythe's face reddened with anger. "Get out of my store this instant," he said to Alex. Turning to Norman, he said, "You, too. Out. Now! And don't come back, or I'll—"

"Not until you give back his ninety-nine dollars and ninety-five cents," Alex interrupted, gesturing toward Norman. With a wave in Ray's direction, she added, "*And* his seventy-nine dollars and ninety-five cents. And all the *others*, Mr. St. Smythe. How many are there, anyway?"

Mr. St. Smythe's mouth dropped open and his eyes grew large as he looked at Norman, then Ray, and back at Alex again. "How did you—er, I mean—what the devil are you talking about?"

"Are you going to give it back, Mr. St. Smythe?" she asked.

"I-I-I refuse to dignify that question with a response!" he sputtered.

"In that case . . ." Alex waved an arm slightly.

A rubber hand rose from its shelf and flew through the air to slap Mr. St. Smythe in the face with a noisy *thwack!* Mr. St. Smythe staggered back a step as the rubber hand dropped to the counter.

Everyone in the store gasped simultaneously.

Mr. Jackson began to look a bit concerned.

"Well, Mr. St. Smythe, are you going to give these boys their money back or not?" Alex asked.

"Well, I don't . . . I-I mean, I didn't . . ."

The rubber hand rose from the counter, and Mr. St. Smythe ducked with a pathetic cry of fright. But the hand ignored him; instead, it swept over the shelf behind him, knocking several decks of playing cards and tarot cards to the floor. Then it dropped to the counter again.

Mr. Jackson began to back away from the hand, staring at it cautiously as he said, over and over, "Uuhhh . . . this is, um, y'know . . . this is really kind of . . . *creepy.*"

"That is quite enough!" Mr. St. Smythe barked. "You will leave this instant, or I will call the police!"

"Do you think the police would like to hear about how you and your employees have been stealing money from the young people of Paradise Valley ever since you opened your store?" Alex asked firmly.

"But that's just . . . that-that-that's . . ." Mr. St. Smythe did not finish his sentence. He stared open-mouthed at Alex. From the tense expression on Mr. St. Smythe's face, Ray knew the man was thinking hard, trying to come up with a way to handle this sudden unpleasant situation, which could possibly topple his little moneymaking scam and get him in trouble with the police, as well.

"I don't think you understand yet, Mr. St. Smythe," Alex said. "I'm not leaving here until you give these boys their money back."

Alex pointed to the cash register. A short bolt of electricity shot from her index finger and zapped the register. A few sparks sputtered from the machine's keyboard, and the cash drawer popped open hard, jangling the coins inside.

Mr. St. Smythe looked as if he were about to shout at her, but then something else happened.

One-dollar bills, fives, tens, and twenties began to shoot out of the cash drawer and into the air, then flutter downward lazily. Coins scattered upward, then rained musically to the counter and the floor. The customers in the store suddenly lunged forward, groping for the bills fluttering through the air.

"Stop!" Mr. St. Smythe boomed at them. "Do not touch anything! In fact . . . everyone out. Now! Out of the store. We're *closed!*"

The customers were so preoccupied with the money scattered all over the floor that Mr. Jackson had to herd them to the door and out onto the sidewalk like cattle. Only Ray, Norman, Alex, Mr. St. Smythe, and Mr. Jackson remained.

Then the smarmy redheaded employee appeared from the back of the store. He looked around and asked, "Hey . . . what's going on?"

"Oh, shut up, Leland!" Mr. St. Smythe snapped. He took in a deep breath and shouted, "Burke! Mr. Burke! Get out here!"

The huge man hurried from the back of the store to the counter, looking around at the mess with a bemused expression.

"Get that crazy woman out of this store, Mr. Burke!" Mr. St. Smythe demanded, pointing at Alex. *"Immediately!"*

Mr. Burke turned on Alex slowly, his shoulders slightly hunched.

Ray remembered that Alex had referred to him as Mr. St. Smythe's "gorilla." That was exactly how Mr. Burke appeared as he made his way toward Alex, his shoulders slightly hunched, fingers curled into fists, head lowered and chin jutting. Ray found it difficult not to smile, because he knew exactly what Mr. Burke was walking into.

Mr. Burke was walking into Alex's magnetic force field!

The big man staggered backward slightly, then moved forward again. He staggered backward a second time. He didn't try to move forward again. Instead, he stood frozen in place, looking flustered and a little worried. Mr. Burke turned, very slowly, to Mr. St. Smythe.

"Well, what are you waiting for, imbecile?" Mr. St. Smythe barked.

Mr. Burke turned to Alex again. He took in a deep breath, braced himself, then rushed toward her.

This time, there was no magnetic force field!

Ray flinched as he watched the big man bumble forward without resistance, quickly gaining momentum. Alex stepped aside and Mr. Burke whizzed by her like a cannonball, picking up speed until he slammed into a shelf of rubber toys. Then he fell backward onto the floor, dazed.

Rubber balls, rubber spiders, rubber cubes, rubber shrunken heads . . . they all fell to the floor and bounced around for a moment. The spiders and cubes and heads eventually came to rest, but the little rubber balls just kept bouncing and bouncing, all over the place, against walls and shelves and the counter.

One of the little rubber balls bounced off Mr. St. Smythe's pink and sweaty forehead. Mr. Burke lay on the floor, propped up on one elbow, shaking his head and rubbing a big hand over his face.

Mr. St. Smythe's fleshy cheeks quivered as he clenched his teeth and turned to his silver-toothed employee. "Mr. Jackson," he hissed. "Call the police!"

"What?" Mr. Jackson replied. "I'm not so sure that's a good idea, Mr. St. Smythe. I mean, what with the—"

"I *said*, call the *police!* This is-is-is *insane!* Don't worry, I'll take care of everything, Mr. Jackson. Just call the police *now!*"

Mr. Jackson went to a phone on the wall behind the counter and made the call.

Ray tensed. Now that the police were being called, the rest of Alex's plan had to happen quickly. He prepared himself to go through with the next few steps.

Mr. Burke struggled to sit up. Rubber bugs were scattered all over him, and the second he saw them, he cringed as he slapped them off. He leaned against the shelves for balance as he tried to get up.

Above Mr. Burke, one of the trick boxes had been jarred to the very edge of its shelf. Mr. Burke's weight against the shelves disturbed the box even more, and it dropped onto his head, knocking him to the floor again, even more dazed than before.

Slowly, Mr. St. Smythe turned to Alex, frowning.

"There's money all around you, Mr. St. Smythe," Alex said. "Do you mean to tell me you're not going to return the money you've stolen from these two boys?"

Mr. St. Smythe stepped toward Alex and spoke just above a whisper. "I did not *steal* it from them. They gave it to me."

When Alex replied, her voice was so low, Ray had to strain to hear her words.

"So, you admit it," she said. "*That*, Mr. St. Smythe, is all I needed to hear."

"I admit that those two boys were careless and unwise—nothing more."

"But you and your employees lied to them, and to all the other young people you've fooled into giving you money," Alex said, standing her ground. "You made promises you never intended to keep, and you took money you never intended to earn."

Suddenly, a violent storm struck inside St. Smythe's Magic Emporium. Merchandise began to fly from the shelves. Brightly painted boxes, "floating" balls, trick bouquets, collapsible knives, rubber chickens, open containers stuffed with glittery feathers, magic hats, clangy chains of large shiny rings, a dozen plastic, red-gummed chattering teeth, and so much more. It all hit the floor and bounced and scattered and fluttered around. The sound of all the tumbling, crashing merchandise rose like thunder in the store!

Leland opened his mouth and released a high, shrill scream. He spun around, ran to the back of the store, and disappeared down the corridor.

The store looked like David Copperfield's road tour bus had exploded.

"No!" Mr. St. Smythe shouted. "Nooo! That's my merchandise."

"These boys aren't merchandise, Mr. St. Smythe!" Alex snapped. "Give back their money."

All the spilled goods finished rolling and skittering around and fell silent. The only sound left was the brittle *clackety-clack* of the plastic chattering teeth that jittered around on the floor as if looking for something to bite.

Mr. St. Smythe said, "I'll do no such thing!"

That was when Ray saw the patrol car pull up to the curb outside. Paradise Valley was a small town, and it didn't take the police long to get anywhere. Ray turned to Alex and gave her a single slight nod.

"Fine, then," Alex said, and there was a threatening note in her voice. She raised her hand and pointed her index finger directly at Mr. St. Smythe.

Mr. St. Smythe's angry scowl quickly melted

away. He tossed a quick glance at the cash register. Thin wisps of smoke were still rising from the keyboard. Looking fearfully at her finger again, Mr. St. Smythe took a step back and held an arm protectively over his face.

"Nooo, plee-ee-ee-eeze!" he squealed.

Mr. Jackson ducked behind the counter.

A bolt of electricity shot from Alex's finger and sliced through the air. It looked like it was heading directly for Mr. St. Smythe, but instead it zapped one of the glittery feathers that was fluttering down to the floor. The feather went up in a little puff of smoke.

As soon as Ray saw the doors of the patrol car pop open, he hurried out the door. "Excuse me, officers," Ray said as the two policemen approached. "There's something going on here that I think you should know about."

As Ray spoke to the police officers, the mess inside the store appeared to be cleaning itself up. Merchandise flew back to its place on the shelves rapidly as Mr. St. Smythe watched in shock.

"How-how-how . . . do you d-d-*do* that?" Mr. St. Smythe whimpered in a voice high with frustration and fear as he looked at the mysterious Gypsy woman again.

But she was gone.

"Hey!" Mr. St. Smythe said. He rushed to the spot where she'd been standing just a couple heartbeats ago. "Whuh-where did she go?"

Norman spun around to see that the Gypsy woman was, indeed, gone. His back had been turned when she left, just as it had been when she entered.

The door opened and the two police officers walked into the store, followed closely by Ray. "He's the one," Ray said, pointing at Norman.

"What?" Norman asked, looking very worried. "What did *I* do?"

"Nothing, Norm," Ray said. "I was just telling these officers here that you got ripped off just like I did."

"Oh, thank goodness you're here!" Mr. St. Smythe gasped as he hurried toward the officers. "Just a moment ago—not five seconds ago—that woman—"

"What woman?" one of the officers asked.

"Well, she was there. She was right there!"

"*Who* was right there?" the other officer asked.

"That-that-that . . . *witch!* That *sorceress!*" Mr. St. Smythe stammered, pointing at the place where the Gypsy woman had been standing. "She made everything fly off the shelves! The place was a mess! She-she-she . . . hexed my cash register!"

The police officers gave one another odd looks, then turned to Norman.

"You paid to be in this magic club, too?" the first officer asked.

"Yep," Norman said, nodding emphatically. "I gave Mr. St. Smythe here about a hundred dollars last night. But today, he acted like he'd never seen me before, and they tried to kick me out of the store."

"Who took your money?" the other officer asked.

Norman raised an arm and pointed a stiff finger at Mr. St. Smythe. "Him. The owner."

The officers nodded, then one of them looked around and said, "The place looks kind of empty. Anybody else here?"

Ray stepped over to the counter, leaned forward, and pointed downward to where Mr. Jackson cowered. "This guy," he said. "And there's another guy in the back room. His name's Leland. And that's Mr. Burke," he added, pointing to the hulking man on the floor.

The officers stepped forward and looked over the counter at Mr. Jackson, who was still huddling there. "Would you mind standing up, sir?" one of the officers said.

Mr. Jackson slowly rose from behind the counter.

"B-but wait!" Mr. St. Smythe blurted. "What about that woman? What about all the damage she did to my store? She came in here and everything went crazy. My merchandise was scattered everywhere."

"There doesn't appear to be any woman here now," the second officer said, looking around. "And your store seems to be just fine. I think maybe we should discuss what these two boys have said about you and your employees."

Mr. St. Smythe sneered down at Ray and Norman. "I have no doubt these two hooligans had something to do with that woman. Especially him!" he said, pointing at Ray. "I've had trouble with him before."

"What kind of trouble?" the first officer asked.

Mr. St. Smythe's mouth opened and closed a few times, but nothing came out. He ran a hand over his balding head nervously. "Well, I . . ." Mr. St. Smythe said, but he didn't seem able to finish. He simply released a long sigh.

"I think we need to have a word with you, sir," the first police officer said, "down at the station."

Ray looked at Norman, and the two boys grinned at one another.

CHAPTER 12

Ray left the St. Smythe Magic Emporium and headed to the police station with Norman. There the boys told their stories to one of the officers while Mr. St. Smythe, Mr. Burke, Mr. Jackson, and Leland were being questioned somewhere else in the station.

One of the officers called Mr. Alvarado, who drove to the station to pick up Ray. On the way home, Ray told him about everything—including the twenty-dollar bill he'd filched. He didn't tell his dad about Alex's involvement, however; for her sake that had to remain a secret.

"I'm sorry, Dad, I really am," Ray said. "I saw my name on the envelope and thought maybe you'd changed your mind about helping me out with some money. But that's not an excuse. I should've asked first, and I'm sorry I didn't. I mean, even if you had decided to give me some money, it wouldn't have been a hundred dollars. I should've known."

Mr. Alvarado sighed. "Well, yes, you're right, you should have known. Not that it happens often at our place, but anytime you find money around the house, it's a good idea to speak up before you take it. I'm glad you recognize that, though, and glad that you've told me. But I'm afraid it wouldn't have happened if I'd only put that money away, where it belonged."

"What was it for?" Ray asked.

"You weren't supposed to know, but . . . that was your birthday money. I've been saving up for your bike. Charlie found me a deal on the transmission, so it wasn't as expensive as I'd expected. I put the money I'd saved toward your bike in the envelope with the other money I'd saved. Then the telephone rang and I guess I forgot to put the money away afterward. Sorry to spoil the surprise for you."

Ray brightened a little. "Really? A bike?" He laughed. "That's what *I* was saving for before I . . . well, before I met Mr. St. Smythe."

"Yes, I know. And your punishment for all this is to keep reminding yourself how hard you worked for that money, and how quickly and easily it disappeared. Think about that the next time you spend money on something."

Ray nodded, then muttered, "I don't know what I was thinking."

"Oh, don't be too hard on yourself. It happens to everybody at one time or another. But it only needs to happen once," Mr. Alvarado added with a smile. "Now, how does pizza sound?"

"Sounds great, Dad," Ray said. He was feeling better already.

Later that night, Alex was glad to hear the doorbell ring. She hoped it was Ray. The silence between her and Annie was growing old, and Alex wanted someone in the house she could talk to.

When she opened the door, she burst into a peal of laughter. Ray stood on the porch wearing a huge sombrero. It was a bit too big for his head and fell all the way to his eyebrows. "Are you making a run for the border?" Alex asked.

"Very funny," Ray said as he stepped inside. The hat barely fit through the door. "Is Annie home?"

"Annie?" Alex asked, wrinkling her nose. "You

came here to see Annie? Wearing a sombrero? I don't think she's going to want to do a hat dance with you. She's barely speaking these days."

"Okay, you can cut out the jokes now. Is she around?"

"She's in the bedroom."

"Could you get her?"

"Get her? She's not even talking to me."

"Okay, let's go."

Ray started for the bedroom with Alex right behind him. "Hey, Ray . . . what's going on here?"

"You'll see," he said, adding, "My turn to keep secrets." He stopped outside the bedroom and knocked on the door. "Annie? Are you in there?"

After a long pause, Annie said, "Ray? Is that you?"

"Yes, can I come in?"

"Well, yeah, but . . . what for?"

Ray opened the door and stepped into the room. Annie was sitting on the edge of her bed with the telephone receiver held to her ear. She looked up at Ray with an odd expression. "Ray," she said, "did you get a job delivering tacos or something?"

Ray turned to Alex, who was still standing in the hall, and beckoned her forward. "C'mon," he said. "This is for both of you."

When Alex stepped into the room, Annie said

into the phone, "Can I call you back? I've got company. . . . Okay, see ya." She hung up the phone and stood to face them. "All right, what's going on?" she asked suspiciously.

"Sit there on the bed, both of you," Ray said.

"What're you up to, Ray?" Alex asked.

"I'm gonna do a magic trick for you," he replied.

"A magic trick?" Alex rolled her eyes. "Haven't we had enough magic for a while, Ray?"

"Just sit down and watch," he said impatiently.

Alex and Annie exchanged a long, silent stare, then sat down on the bed stiffly, but not too close together.

"Okay," Ray said. "As you can see, I'm wearing this old sombrero of my dad's. That's because I couldn't find a top hat. Most magicians wear top hats, but this is the best I could do, so just work with me, okay?"

The girls stared at him unresponsively.

"Okay?"

They nodded.

"Hey, you guys need to loosen up," Ray said, shaking his head. "I mean, I'm not gonna saw either of you in half, so relax."

He reached up, grabbed the crown of the sombrero between the thumb and fingers of his right hand, and took off the hat. As he spoke, he passed the hat from one hand to the other and back again.

"As you can see," Ray said, "this is an ordinary sombrero, the kind any tourist might buy on a visit to Mexico or to any of the cities near its border. As it happens, my dad won this one knocking milk bottles over with baseballs at a carnival. However . . ."

He removed a pencil from his pocket as he turned the sombrero upside down before him. Over the upended hat, he made circular motions with the pencil.

"With a few waves of my magic wand," Ray continued, "this ordinary sombrero becomes—"

"That's a pencil," Annie said.

Ray stopped moving the pencil and sighed. "It was a pencil," he said. "And it'll be a pencil again tomorrow. But right *now*, it's a magic wand."

"Okay," Annie said with a shrug.

"With a few waves of my magic wand," he said again, "this ordinary sombrero becomes . . . a magic hat!"

Ray tossed the pencil over his shoulder, reached into the sombrero's crown, and pulled something out. He held it before him with a big grin on his face, and sang, "Tah-daahhh!"

Alex and Annie gasped at the same instant.

Annie blurted, "My sweater!" at the same moment Alex exclaimed, "Your sweater!" They jumped up, and Annie took the sweater from Ray.

"Where did you *find* it?" Alex asked.

"Don't tell me *you* stole it?" Annie said. "What would you want with my sweater, Ray?"

Ray laughed. "No, I didn't steal it. But neither did Alex."

"Then where did it come from?" Annie asked.

"You said you put it on Annie's bed with a bunch of stacked and folded clothes, right, Alex?" Ray asked.

"Yeah," Alex said. "Then it just disappeared."

"Along with all those clothes," Ray added. He turned to Annie and asked, "Did you send some clothes down to the Re-Run Thrift Store recently?"

"Yes," she replied. "I do every fall."

"We all do," Alex said. "Every year, Mom has us round up the clothes we don't want anymore, and she takes them down there."

"Well, that's where I found your sweater," Ray said to Annie, looking rather impressed with himself.

Annie frowned. "You mean *Mom* took my sweater?"

"Not on purpose, Annie!" Alex replied. "It was *my* fault. I should've known why all those clothes were stacked on your bed, and I should've put the sweater someplace else. I'm sorry, Annie."

Annie turned to Alex slowly. She looked very serious. *"You're* sorry? You don't have anything to be sorry about, Alex. *I'm* sorry! All this time I've been accusing you of stealing my sweater, and the whole time—well, I guess I knew better. I was just so upset about losing my favorite sweater, I ended up taking it out on you."

Alex smiled. "So, if something disappears from your wardrobe again, you're not gonna blame me?"

"Definitely not," Annie said, throwing her arms around Alex. The girls hugged for a long moment.

"Just call me the Amazing Ray!"

The girls laughed, then Alex asked, "What's the story with Mr. St. Smythe and his band of merry thieves?"

Ray said, "Well, when Dad and I got back from dinner, there was a message on the answering machine from one of the police officers. It turns out that Mr. St. Smythe is *not* Mr. St. Smythe, at all. He's got nine different identities, and he's wanted in six states! In fact, he's not even British! He's from Arkansas, for crying out loud!"

"No way!" Alex exclaimed. "What about the others?"

"Mr. Burke is an ex-convict," Ray said. "He's broken his probation by leaving the state of Texas, and he'll be going back there very soon, for a nice long visit. Mr. Jackson and Leland have worked with Mr. St. Smythe before, and the authorities in three other states are very interested in getting their hands on them."

"Are you going to get your money back?" Alex asked.

"Eventually," Ray said. "But everything's okay with Dad. I told him the whole story and he was really cool about it."

"You told him *everything?*" Alex asked, her eyes widening.

"No, no . . . nothing about you. Just everything else."

"Ray," Annie said, "thank you so much for doing this. I really appreciate it."

"I guess you've redeemed yourself," Alex said to Ray with a mock scowl. "Next time you do such a crazy thing, I'm gonna . . . I'm gonna . . ."

"You're gonna what?" Ray challenged.

Alex saw the sombrero lying on the bed. She telekinetically thought it up onto Ray's head and gave it a firm tug. It plunked down over his eyes and he groped blindly around the room until he fell face first with a shout and a laugh onto the bed.

"That's just a little taste of what you can look forward to if you get yourself in that kind of trouble again. No more hocus pocus, okay?" Alex said.

"Are you kidding?" Ray said, taking off the hat. "This whole mess has made my interest in magic . . . disappear."

About the Author

Joseph Locke is the author of nine previous novels for young readers, including *Kiss of Death* and *Game Over.* He lives with his wife, Logan, and their dog, Tucker, on a wombat farm in northern California. He is currently at work on an unauthorized autobiography; the moment it's published, he plans to sue himself for big bucks.

Sometimes, it takes a kid to solve a good crime....

Original stories based on the hit Nickelodeon show!

#1 A Slash in the Night
by Alan Goodman

#2 Takeout Stakeout
By Diana G. Gallagher

#3 Hot Rock
by John Peel

#4 Rock 'n' Roll Robbery
by Lydia C. Marano and David Cody Weiss

(Coming in mid-October 1997)

To find out more about *The Mystery Files of Shelby Woo* or any other Nickelodeon show, visit Nickelodeon Online on America Online (Keyword: NICK) or send e-mail (NickMailDD@aol.com).

Published by Pocket Books

1338-02